DANGEROUS FALLS AHEAD

DANGEROUS FALLS AHEAD

An Adirondack Canoeing Adventure

by
Liza Frenette

Illustrated by
Jane Gillis

North Country Books, Inc.
Utica, New York

DANGEROUS FALLS AHEAD
An Adirondack Canoeing Adventure

ISBN 0-925168-79-3

Library of Congress Cataloging-in-Publication Data

Frenette, Liza, 1958-
    Dangerous falls ahead: an Adirondack canoeing adventure / Liza
Frenette; illustrated by Jane Gillis.— 1st ed.
       p. cm.
    Summary: On a canoe trip with her father and friends in the Adiron-
dack Mountains, eleven-year-old Bridget discovers both the fun and
danger of the woods and water.
    ISBN 0-925168-79-3 (pbk.)
    [1. Canoes and canoeing—Fiction. 2. Camping—Fiction. 3.
Rivers—Fiction. 4. Adirondack Mountains (N.Y.)—Fiction.]
    I. Gillis, Jane, ill. II. Title.

PZ7.F88935 Dan 2001
[Fic]—dc21   2001030987

North Country Books, Inc.
311 Turner Street
Utica, New York 13501

This book is dedicated to my brother,
Michael Frenette,
who spent thirteen summers at Raquette Falls
as the caretaker for the
Department of Environmental Conservation,
allowing me, my daughter, and assorted
friends and family members
many wonderful moments
with the waterfalls, the fireflies,
the deer, the walks, the hammock,
and some awesome breakfasts on the
screened porch.

It is also dedicated to my parents,
Jim and Susie Hull Frenette.
My dad has paddled from Long Lake to Tupper Lake
about a gazillion times, and
provided me with some great maps, books, puns, and insight.
My mom, a quilt artist, is the inspiration for the
quilts in my books,
for that is how she tells her stories.

Contents

Acknowledgments

There are always many people to thank when a creative project goes from being grains of sand to a sandcastle. Without these people, it would not have turned out the same, or maybe not at all. It might, in fact, have been washed away by the tides without them.

To God, whose Spirit of the woods and sky stays with me.

To the brave souls who once paddled the Raquette River trip with me, and lived to tell the tale: Ellen Frenette, Mike Frenette, and Rob Gillis; and later, Ray and Lori Martin, who never did get that last soda.

To Gracey Meagher Frenette, for being who she is, for helping me with the book, and for a glorious day doing research at Raquette Falls.

To Alyssa Schultz, who helped me with many details of the book, aided by contributions from Erica, Corrin, and Abigail Schultz. Thanks for some great lake time, too. To Gary Schultz for tourist information.

To Ranger Ben Woodard, for throwing out the rope on a hot summer day.

To fellow writers who helped tremendously with the revisions on this manuscript, Claudia Ricci and Peggy Woods.

To Felice Wallach, for her reminders of my strengths.

To my tribe, many of whom help me find places to swim, or at the very least, keep me from sinking: Lori Martin, Jane Filowat, Charlie Miller, Diane Cyr, Karen Sleight, Gerry Colborn, Claudia Ricci, Rosie Guidice, Linda Hogan, Liz Jagger, Ellen Hollander, George Moore, Jackie Simond, Anna Janowski, Pam Sager, Amy Biancolli, Chris Ringwald, Sue Okun, Peter Bogart, James Ryan, Mary Bergquist, Linda Hamell, and Rob Devlin. Oh yeah, and Tony, for gum.

To some great writing professors at the State University of New York at Morrisville and at Albany, who taught me about deadlines and creativity.

To Charles W. Bryan, Jr.'s book, *Raquette River of the Forest*, for some wonderful information about the Raquette River and Long Lake.

To the Adirondack Museum in Blue Mountain Lake for preserving Noah John Rondeau's cabin and stories.

To some special paddlers and swimmers who light up my life: Willie and Charlie Bencze, Bridget and Gretchen O'Leary; Jamie Frenette; Gracey, Peter, and Annie Frenette. To Sara, Susie, and Michael Heidinger, who are starting their own adventures.

To Danielle DerOhannesan, who loves Ming so dearly and always reminds me of how lucky I am.

To Bill Doolittle, the best editor and mentor.

To Nick Burns, for his assistance with this project.

To my uncle Lou Simmons, who inspired me with his writing and his artwork.

To Jasmine, my family, who knows about the contentment of a good book, sparkles when she swims, and shared many adventures in the woods with me that we turned into song.

Chapter One

The Sweat

The sweat is so gross. It slimes the back of my neck and makes my forehead oily, which makes my bangs stick to me. I try to blow them away from my skin by pushing my breath upward with my bottom lip out, but then I just feel my hot breath and that's gross, too. The windows are rolled down in the truck, but outside the air is muggy, so it feels like this paste is covering my skin. Ugh.

I just wish my dad would get air conditioning in his truck; everybody has air conditioning, but dad said there are not enough hot days in summer in the Adirondacks and it's just not worth the extra money.

I can't wait, I simply can't wait, to get in the water and cool off; even though I can't possibly wear the dorky bathing suit that mom bought me. Ugh. How could she have bought me a swimsuit with ruffles that's more for a little girl playing on a beach? I need a suit for a real swimmer! She brought it home yesterday and when she took it out of the bag I said I couldn't possibly wear it. She said it would have to do because there was no time now to take it back to the store before this canoe trip. Well, I will wear my shorts and a t-shirt, that's all there is to it.

Just thinking about it makes me squirm because I want to get in the lake and cool off so much.

"Dad, how much longer until we get to Long Lake?"

"Bridget, you just asked ten minutes ago. We haven't even been on the road all that long."

"Well, I know, but I got all hot loading up the truck with everything. Now I'm just hot and staying that way."

"Well, we're in Tupper Lake right now, and Long Lake is the next town," he said.

"Can we stop at that gas station?" I asked. "I have to go the bathroom."

My dad pulled in. From where we were, we could see the lake just down the road. There was an ice cream stand on the side of the gas station store, and I didn't even have to ask. My dad just looked at me, smiled, and said, "What kind do you want?" He got the ice cream while I used the restroom. They had all these special flavors I'd never tried before. I got bubble gum. It was really good. It seemed like there were sparkles in the ice cream that had little bursts of bubble gum tastes.

While we were standing outside the truck licking our ice cream cones, Ming, my little dog, woke up in the truck and put her paws on the edge of the rolled-down window. She was staring at my ice cream. Ming loves to eat. If you even go in the kitchen at home, she'll wake up from a sound sleep and prance on in, hoping for some food. She's a little black-and-white Shih Tzu that my mom got me a little less than a year ago. I got to pick out the name, and I picked Ming because I read that Shih Tzu's were bred for royalty during the Ming Dynasty. I read a lot about dogs before getting one because I'd wanted one for so long. Besides, I love to read.

Dad wasn't sure about bringing her along, but Ming is my buddy and she goes most everywhere I do, except school of course. She minds really well, and she knows how to swim. I've taken her in the canoe quite a few times this summer, out on Moose Pond near where I live with my mom. She's really good in the boat.

Before I finished my cone, I saved the last bite for her. She gobbled it right up, licking every last drop. "Will we paddle by here at the end of our trip?" I asked my dad, pointing to the lake.

"Not quite," he said. "We're going to end up at a boat launch before Tupper Lake on the Raquette River, instead of coming all the way into town. Otherwise, we'd have about another fourteen miles of paddling. I think our route is going to be long enough, especially since we all have different paddling skills," he said.

Anna, Gracey, their dad, and Gracey's friend Peter are coming on the trip with my dad and me. Anna is my best friend, and she's also my neighbor; she's eleven, like me. Gracey is her sister, and she's six. Our families are friends. We're going to meet them at the boat launch in Long Lake and then head out on a canoe trip that will be a little over thirty miles from Long Lake to just outside Tupper Lake in the Adirondack Mountains, where we all live.

"Your mom and Anna's mom will wait for us at Axton Landing

on the last day of our trip, sometime in the middle of the afternoon. They're going to bring a picnic and relax, since it's hard to give an exact time when we'll arrive," my dad said.

As we went to get back into the truck, I noticed a square blue sign on a pole at the street corner. It said Tourist Information. Underneath it was another sign that said Long Lake 22.

"Hey, Dad," I said. "Are we tourists now?"

"Not really, because we live around here," he said. He looked at the sign and smiled.

"Bridget, that sign doesn't just mean what you think it does, that there's a place for tourists to get information."

I smiled. My dad loves to make up stories about road signs.

"It means this is a place where you get information ABOUT tourists!" he said.

"Like what?" I asked.

"Oh, like where they're from and what's their favorite ice cream, and of course, the most important part, do they have any secrets? You know, tourist information," he said. "Because everybody has a story to tell."

"Well, if we see any tourists, we'll have to be sure to talk to them now," I said, smiling. A lot of tourists come to the Adirondacks because it's so beautiful. There are plenty of mountains and lakes.

"Do we stay on this road the whole way to Long Lake?" I asked my dad.

He leaned over me to open the glove compartment. He yanked out a map.

4

I should have known. I should've kept quiet. Every time I ask anything in the car about location or direction my dad pulls out a map and makes me look up where we are and find the town we're going to. He'll say, "Is that north, south, east, or west of where we are?" Or, "Are we near a lake or a river? Find that on the map. It's always good to know where the water is in case you want to go for a swim or a paddle. Plus finding the water on the map is a good way to get your bearings."

It's no wonder my dad became a teacher. Everything is a lesson waiting to happen.

I unfolded the New York State map and looked high up in the top part of the state. I know that much from my little bit of map reading. We live in northern New York, in the Adirondack Mountains, which is a big green blob on the map. My mom and I live on the backside of Whiteface Mountain, in the town of Wilmington, and my dad lives nearby in Saranac Lake. They're divorced. Right now, I'm spending a couple weeks with my dad, and the first part of our summer vacation is this canoe trip.

I found Long Lake on the map, and saw that it is both a big lake and a little town. I followed the lake with my finger, tracing the little blue puddle on the map until it narrowed at one end to a stringy, curvy blue line that said Raquette River in sideways letters along the river. I had to turn the map to read it. The squiggly blue line spilled out into another huge puddle, which was Tupper Lake. We were going to camp one night on Long Lake and then one night at Raquette Falls, which is where you have to carry your boats and stuff a mile around these dangerous waterfalls that are part of the Raquette River.

"Hey, this doesn't look too far at all," I said.

"Yeah, no sweat," my father replied.

"Yes, sweat," I said, "remember, I'm already sweating." I lifted my bangs off my forehead. "I HAVE to swim before we get in the canoe. Besides, I know Anna will want to go swimming, too. I told her we could go before we started the trip."

"Well, we'll see," my father said.

I twisted in my seat and looked out the back window of the truck again to see if Anna's dad had caught up to us yet.

"Hey, there they are!" I shouted, waving. "It's them."

Even with the canoe in back, the top of it resting on the cab of our truck, I could see Anna in the front seat of her parents' station wagon behind us. Their canoe was on racks on top of their car. Anna waved back. Her dad waved. Gracey and Peter were in the back seat, so I couldn't really see them, that is, until Peter saw everybody waving and he tried to stick his head up and make goofy faces at me.

I laughed and turned back around. I was so excited about this trip. We'd been planning it all summer.

And Anna and I have our own plans for the trip, too. When we get to Raquette Falls, we're going to camp in our own little tent, away from the others, at the edge of a big meadow my dad said was there. It would be like camping out by ourselves, and my dad said we were big enough now to do that. But we have some secret plans for that night that no one else knows about but Anna and me.

Chapter Two

Signs

Ming was panting big time, which made me realize she was still hot, so I got out the thermos of water I always keep for her.

"See Dad, even Ming is suffocating from the heat. You should really get air conditioning. You still have the whole month of August ahead and you know August is always hot," I said. "Besides, if it doesn't rain, it will never cool off and you'll be sorry you don't have a cool truck."

He just smiled and tapped the steering wheel. He was listening to some oldies music tape.

I poured Ming some water in the cap of the thermos. She gulped it right down.

"I brought a little cushion so Ming can lay under my canoe seat if the sun gets too hot," I told my dad.

"Good idea," he said.

I picked up my puppy and she put her head in the crook of my arm. She loves to do that. She's so cute. She has long hair, and some parts are coal black and others are pure white. She is a kind of dog that has hair, rather than fur, which is better for people with allergies to animals. Like me, I'm allergic to cats and they make me sneeze and make my eyes water. But Ming doesn't do that. Ming's eyes are pools of shining black. Sometimes they look like ink. She gave a big sigh, put her face into the hot breeze from the window, and we both settled back for the rest of the ride.

The drive from Tupper Lake to Long Lake is beautiful. There are no houses, stop signs, traffic lights, or stores. It's all trees—big tall evergreens, mostly. The road looks like a river between all those trees. After awhile, we could see mountains straight ahead of us. It looked like we'd be driving right through them if we drove far enough.

"That's the Santanoni Range," my dad said, nodding to the mountains.

I hoped he wouldn't make me find them on the map.

We drove through Long Lake, which really seemed like two separate towns, because there are all these shops on one street and then you go up this big curvy hill into another part of the town. As soon as you come into town, you can see the lake, which was bright blue in the sunshine. I saw a neon-yellow seaplane landing on the lake, next to a sign that advertised seaplane rides.

"Hey, Dad, can we do that sometime? Take a ride over the lake and mountains?" I asked.

"That sounds like something great for next year, Bridget," he said. "Only you won't be able to bring Ming on that trip."

I didn't think Ming would like flying too much, either. But I sure would love to try it. In a little airplane like that, I bet I'd feel like a bird. Maybe I'd feel like a bald eagle, or an osprey—something big and powerful like that. I turned back away from the lake as we drove by an old hotel and an old general store, and instead of turning up the big hill, we headed straight on the road to the boat launch.

"Hey look," my father said, pointing. "There's a new sign for us. Snowplow Turn."

"What do you think that one means?" I asked.

Right away, he said, "Oh well, it's a sign to say be on the lookout for a rare and really strange looking bird." His voice changed, and got very serious, and I knew he was about to tell one of his stories. "It's a snowplow tern! It has wings like the wings on a snowplow, so it's clumsy looking. And it's a yellow bird, of course, like your mom's plow."

My mom works in a snowplow for her job. She sits next to the driver and moves the wing plow on the side of a big yellow plow truck to clear the sides of the road from snow in the winter. The driver moves the plow in the front. My mom works for the Department of Transportation.

I laughed at the thought of a bird looking like a snowplow.

"Of course," my dad said, "Terns are actually shorebirds, and you're most likely to see them at the ocean. Their name is really spelled t-e-r-n. But, hey, if this bird is weird enough to look like a snowplow, it could have a weird spelling, too," he said.

"Sure!" I said. "Maybe because it's a mountain tern, it has a different spelling, which is t-u-r-n! That makes it different from an ocean tern!"

The thing is, when my dad starts telling me stories about signs, they just start to seem real. I mean, why couldn't they be? A lot of things have more than one meaning. With my dad, it's almost like he knows these secret codes.

I couldn't help it. I looked up, just to see if some big yellow bird might be circling around. The sky was blue and empty of anything but clear white clouds. I tried to find one cloud that might be in the shape of an odd bird, which could possibly be our special snowplow turn. But I didn't see anything like that.

Clouds are special. You can see a lot of things in clouds. It's almost like a secret message, because not that many people look up very much. Maybe my dad's specialty is finding messages in signs, and mine is with clouds. The best thing to do is to lie in the grass, or float in the water, and just look at the clouds. You can always find something in their shapes.

The coolest thing I ever saw was one big cloud with a trail of smaller clouds behind it. They were shaped so that it looked like a mother duck with four ducklings walking behind her. Each cloud had a little piece that looked like a bill on a duck, and the mother cloud even looked like she was walking very proudly.

My dad turned his music down just then. "What do you think the snowplow turn sign means?" he asked, looking over at me. "Do you have your own story for that sign?"

I thought for a while. "Well, maybe it could be a dance step. You know, in gym class this year we learned a lot of different kinds of dances with different turns, like in square dancing or swing dancing. So really I think that sign means to watch out because there's dancers in the woods and they're doing the snowplow turn. Now that's probably a big wide turn, like a plow would make. So the sign means to watch out, because those dancers might make some big turns and end up out in the road!" I said.

Dad laughed and hit the steering wheel. "That's a great one, Bridget!" he said.

I smiled. I like swapping stories with my father.

And then I looked into the trees we were driving past to see if I could see anything moving in the woods. But not even the leaves on the trees were blowing; it was so still and hot.

I knew that even though I couldn't see any dancers in the woods right now, they would be there soon enough. Anna and I were going to make sure of that. That's why it was so easy for me to think of the story of the dancers for my father, because Anna and I had been talking about dancing for days now. A certain kind of dancing we were going to do in the woods; a secret dance.

Chapter Three

The Bark-eaters

When we reached the boat launch, I let Ming jump out first. She sniffed the air and picked up her nose in the wind blowing off the lake. She was so excited. She started sniffing everywhere.

The breeze felt good. But it wasn't enough. I wanted to swim.

"Dad, can we swim first before we head out?" I asked.

He checked his watch. "I don't think so Bridget. We have to unload the gear and load up the canoes, and it's a long paddle across this lake, believe me, especially with a wind. We won't be doing the whole lake today, but we need to get going so we can be sure and get to one of the lean-tos so we can sleep there tonight."

A lean-to is a place to sleep that's made out of logs on three sides and is open in the front. The roof is high in the front and slopes down in the back. I like to sleep in them because you can fall asleep looking at the woods and the sky.

Right now, though, I needed to swim before the long paddle to the lean-to.

"I have to swim. I'm itchy!" I burst out.

"Itchy?" he said.

"Yeah, sweating makes me itchy. Mom would let us swim," I said.

"Well, your mom never could resist getting wet, that's for sure. But we just don't have time right now for a swim. I promise we'll swim before we sleep tonight. Okay?"

I scowled and turned around. I picked up a couple of flat rocks and skipped them in the lake. My best was three skips. Willie and Charlie, my other neighbors at home, can skip rocks like mad. Willie and Charlie are brothers who are less than a year apart; they're called 'Irish twins.' They're both in my grade. Willie can skip a rock at least ten times, and Charlie, his younger brother, can make a rock skip at least eight times. Of course, they always like to brag about it.

I wished I were a smooth rock right now, skimming over the surface of the lake, or maybe a duck, just diving down into the water. I think it's so funny when ducks stick their butts up in the air when they dive for food. But at least they can get wet whenever they want.

Mom hardly ever says no when I want to swim, even if it's at night. She loves to swim. But she's been away for a few days at a summer quilting class in Massachusetts. Earlier this summer she put her quilts on display in a quilt show in Tupper Lake, and so many people wanted to buy them that she said she was really surprised. So now she wants to learn even more. She makes designs of trees and swans and falling leaves on her quilts. I hope someday she can make me a quilt with Ming on it, using scraps of black and white material.

In the summer, because she's not working in the snowplow, she has a lot more free time. She works part-time doing landscaping for people, usually making rock gardens for them and making flower arrangements in unusual planters. She even made up a business card, and under her name it says "Works with flowers and rocks and moss and crocks." She saves time to take me swimming almost every afternoon, usually with Anna and Gracey.

"Bridget, come on!" my dad said. "You have to help."

I didn't feel like working. I'd already loaded the truck earlier this morning and now it was time to unload it already. Ugh. I just wanted to swim. I bent down and picked up Ming to put her in the truck while I unloaded gear. She licked my cheek. I could tell she was happy. She nuzzled her head into my neck. My bad mood went away.

Just then, Anna, Gracey, their dad, and Peter pulled in behind us.

"Where were you?" I said as they got out of the car. "I thought you were right behind us."

"We had to stop and get candy bars," Gracey said, smiling. "We had marshmallows and graham crackers to make somemores by the campfire tonight, but I left the chocolate bars on the seat in the car and they melted in the sun. So we had to get more."

I ruffled her hair. Somemores are campfire treats that you make with chocolate, marshmallows, and graham crackers. They got the name because when you eat them, you always want some more.

"You sure do keep a good watch on that chocolate," I said. "It's a good thing." One time Gracey and I got lost in a winter snowstorm, and she'd had chocolate chip cookies in her pocket and boy was I glad. It was all we had to eat while we were lost. I'm glad she likes chocolate.

Anna and Gracey's dad unstrapped the canoe off the top of their station wagon, and the rest of us started carrying our gear to the lake—backpacks, sleeping bags, tents, a cooler, and food.

"My dad made me pack three times," I told Anna. "He said I brought way too much stuff for a couple nights, and for being in a canoe, so I had to take out practically everything. But I still snuck in a book. And my teddy bear Lester. And gum and candy."

"I had to use a small pack, too," Anna said. "And then we put everything in plastic bags in case it rains or we get wet."

"Did you get any goodies?" I asked.

"Yeah, I got fireballs so we can dare each other to see who can suck on them the longest, and licorice and caramel creams. And a couple treats for Ming," Anna said.

"Oh, thanks!" I said.

Anna and Gracey love Ming. They keep asking their parents for a dog now that I have one, but their mom doesn't want to get a dog yet, since she just had a baby, Gretchen. She's home with the baby right now, and in three days she's going to ride with my mom to pick us up.

I'm kind of glad they don't have a dog yet, at least for a while, because this way Ming gets a lot more attention. And since I don't have sisters like they do, Ming makes me feel like I have something special.

"Anna, I have to tell you, my mom picked out the WORST bathing suit ever. It's like a little girl's bathing suit. I don't even want to wear it."

17

"How bad can it be?" Anna asked.

I flattened my eyebrows as best as I could, so she would know just how serious this was.

"It has RUFFLES," I said.

Anna looked horrified. "Say no more," she said. "I get the picture."

She looked as grim as I felt.

"Maybe we can cut them off?" she asked hopefully.

"Well, I have my pocket knife, but still, I think that would look worse to have it torn like that," I said. "I don't think pocket knives cut through bathing suit material very well."

"Doesn't it figure this would happen?" Anna asked, as we walked back and forth between the canoes and the vehicles, loading our stuff. "Especially since Willie and Charlie and their older cousin Jamie are going to meet up with us at Raquette Falls tomorrow. You know how Willie and Charlie are always teasing us about things."

Last year they teased me all the time about the snowpants my mother made me wear in the winter, which is something only little kids wear. They teased Anna about her braces, too. I just can't stand how they pick on us. Other times, though, they're really nice, like when they helped find me and Gracey that time we got lost in the woods in the winter. Besides, all our parents are friends, and they thought it'd be this great plan to have them meet us at the waterfalls. Willie and Charlie like to ride horses, so tomorrow they are going to ride horses five miles into Raquette Falls from a ranch.

Their older cousin Jamie is a guide at the ranch. He takes people into the falls for camping and fishing. Willie and Charlie are going to camp with us at the falls and go fishing. They love to fish. One time Willie told me he caught a largemouth bass that was so big it was pulling his canoe, but I don't know if it's a true story.

"Okay, kids, the boats are loaded," my dad shouted just then. "Let's go. Everybody put on life jackets."

I knew this was coming. It was already hot, and we'd have to put on life jackets. Oh, brother.

My dad patted my head. "Don't worry, Bridget, these life jackets are a lot lighter than the old orange ones we had to wear when I was a kid. Those had big, stuffy collars around the necks. They were hot and bulky. At least these are more like vests." He held out mine for me to put on.

I took it, and then Anna and I looked at each other and giggled. Everything was harder when our parents were our age. We'd already figured that out.

We put on the life jackets. Anna got in front of their canoe, her dad got in the back, and Gracey sat in the middle on a cushion on the floor. Peter sat in the middle of our canoe, and put Ming on his lap. He held onto her while she put her paws up on the side of the canoe and sniffed away.

I dipped my paddle in and away we went. My dad and I had paddled a lot this summer to practice for the trip, first on Moose Pond, and then on the Saranac River and on Lower Saranac Lake. Once we canoed on the lake and stayed overnight on one of the islands, camping in our tent. No one else was on the island. It was like we were explorers.

We had the best time!

On our trips, my dad taught me how to move my paddle quickly from one side of the canoe to the other whenever he shouted "Switch," so we could both switch sides at the same time and stay on course better. He also taught me how to do a J stroke when we needed to pull up next to shore or a dock. You move your paddle in the water in the shape of the letter J.

I like to paddle because I like moving through the water so quietly. I like knowing it's just someone else and me moving the boat on our own. My arms do get tired sometimes though. Paddling makes me think of the Mohawk and Algonquin Indians we studied in school this year, who hunted and fished in this part of the Adirondacks before there were any villages or towns. They must have moved so smoothly through the water, scouting for fish and even animals on shore. I wondered what it was like to know if you didn't catch any fish, you wouldn't eat that day.

The name Adirondack is from the Algonquins and it means "Bark-eaters." My dad says that legend has it that sometimes the Indians had to eat bark when they couldn't find any other food. I sure am glad we brought plenty of food, and a couple of fishing poles, too.

Thinking about the bark gave me an idea. I did a J stroke to get the front of our canoe closer to Anna's, and leaned over and whispered to her. Our secret plot for Raquette Falls has to do with an American Indian ceremony, and I just had another idea to add to the plan. When we were done with our own secret ceremony, I told Anna, we would go get Willie and Charlie from their lean-to. And boy, would we have an Indian challenge for them. Seeing how much they liked to brag, Anna and I were quite sure they would have to say yes to our dare!

Chapter Four

Water Songs

Gracey didn't like it that we were whispering.

"What are you guys talking about?" she said. "Please tell me."

I really didn't like to leave her out. "We'll tell you later," I said.

She said she wanted us all to sing some songs. I thought of one Anna and I had learned in music class, and I knew Gracey and Peter would know it because Peter's mom is our music teacher. We all sang loud.

The lake was beautiful. There were other canoes out on the lake, as well as a couple of small sailboats with orange, red, and blue sails. Along the shoreline, we could see camps and some people swimming, and then after awhile, mostly trees. Around us, in the distance, we were surrounded by spruce and hemlocks, maple trees and mountains. My dad kept telling us about the different kinds of trees. I guess teachers never take vacations.

Even though it was breezy, the sun was hot, and I rested my paddle to reach under the seat and get some sunscreen out of the front pocket of my pack. My mom had packed it for me, because I get sunburned easily. I also unfolded my hat, which was scrunched up in the pack, and put that on.

"Peter, will you get us some juice boxes?" I asked.

He reached into our little cooler and got some out. We could only bring a small cooler because we needed to travel light. At the end of Long Lake, we would start down the Raquette River and then have that mile-long carry around the falls. It was going to be a lot of work to haul all our stuff on that trail.

I was really dreading that long carry.

"Tell me that poem about me making breakfast for my little sister Annie," Peter shouted from behind me. I made it up for him one day and now he likes me to tell it to him whenever he comes over to Gracey's house.

> *Little Peter, Little Peter*
> *Was scrambling eggs with a beater*
> *He mixed them so fast they flew up in the air*
> *And landed with a splat in Annie's blonde hair*
> *She gulped them all down, so he did indeed feed her!*

Peter laughed. Then he scooped his hand in the water and splashed some water on my back. "You're silly, Bridget!" he said.

"Well, that's my poem," I said. "Now I used it all up, so I better think of something else for the campfire tonight. You better work on a story, dance, or something else yourself. Remember, tonight we're all supposed to do something by the campfire."

"Oh, I already have an idea, don't you worry about that," Peter said.

"Hey, Bridget, we'll have to make up a new verse for your

Adirondack song. It'll be about paddling from Long Lake to Tupper Lake," my dad said.

Every time we have an adventure, we add a verse to the song. It's something my mom and dad started doing with me when I was little. She started doing it the first time I climbed a mountain, Panther Mountain, between Tupper Lake and Saranac Lake.

"Sing what parts you already have!" Peter said. "Then, at the end of the trip, we can help you make up a new verse about this canoe trip."

So I did, and my dad joined in.

Oh, we are living in the Adirondacks
It feels so good to be here,
'Cause we are living in the Adirondacks
so put your feet up on the cooler and look for deer!
 Oh, Panther Mountain,
 the first mountain Bridget hiked
 We saw ferns and rocks and froggies
 and a view from the top we really liked.
Oh, we're out in the snow in Lake Clear
Skiing down the railroad tracks
Bridget's being pulled on a sled
We've got the wind and the sun at our backs.
 Oh, Little Long Pond
 what'd you do with Bridget's bear?
 He fell off the canoe and disappeared
 He sank to the bottom and he stayed there!
Oh, we are living in the Adirondacks
It feels so good to be here,
'Cause we are living in the Adirondacks,
so put your feet up on the cooler and look for deer!

My dad put his paddle down and clapped.

"What's that part with the bear about?" Peter asked.

"Oh, one time, when I was little, my mom and I went canoeing in the Five Ponds Wilderness Area with a friend of hers and I had this plastic bear in the boat. I always played with it in the bathtub, and I wanted to bring it with me on the trip to swim with. I was playing with him in the water with my hand over the side of the boat and I dropped him and he sank. I was really sad, so my mom made up the verse so we could have a good memory of him."

"Did you ever find him?" Peter asked.

"Nope," I said. "But at least we have the song."

I dug in and paddled some more. After awhile, I realized why they called it Long Lake. It seemed to go on forever. The wind was getting stronger and the waves were big. My arms were getting sore. And I felt this burning kind of feeling in the back of my arms, just below my shoulders.

I was starting to wonder if we would ever get to the lean-to. I knew this was the hardest part of the paddling, being in the open when the wind is roughing up the lake. My dad said the paddling would get easier once we were on the river, because we would go in the same direction as the current. I hoped it would be cooler, too. I suddenly found myself wishing for rain. I wished it would just pour down on us while we were out in our boats and then it would cool us all off and we wouldn't even have to get out of the canoes.

I looked up at the sky. It didn't look like it was even thinking about raining. Not even a little bit. I'd just have to stay hot and sweaty.

Chapter Five

Ashore

"Peter, will you get me a sandwich out of the cooler?" I asked.

"I'm hungry, too," he said.

"Me, too," my dad said from the back of the boat.

We pulled up alongside Anna and Gracey's canoe, and their dad held onto our boat while we all unwrapped sandwiches and took a few minutes to eat. I leaned over and got water to splash on my face.

Gracey squinted into the sun. "How much more?" she asked. "My legs are getting stiff sitting here in the middle of this boat all day."

My dad pulled his canoeing map out of a waterproof bag under his seat. He unfolded it and looked it over.

"Okay, we just passed some islands not too far back," he said. "Now, not too much further up on the right-hand side is a spot called Plumley's Landing. It's named after an old guide from these parts who used to get hired to take people on hunting and fishing trips. He had a camp there at one time. There are a couple of lean-tos there now. I say that's where we'll stop. If the lean-tos are taken, we can always set up our tents at the site."

I finished my sandwich. It was sticking to the roof of my mouth. It was one of my dad's special recipe sandwiches: peanut butter, raisins, wheat germ, and honey. He always makes them for our outdoor adventures. He says they are good energy. I sure needed some right now. But first, I needed water.

Peter handed me the thermos, and I tipped it up and gulped noisily. Then I poured some water from Ming's thermos for her. She drank a whole cup, and then she went back under my seat where it was cool and out of the sun.

"Dad, can I switch places with Peter? I'm tired," I said.

"Well," he replied, squinting into the sun, "I really don't want to take a chance on you two standing up and switching places out here in the middle of the lake. I think you can finish this up today, Bridget, and then Peter can paddle most of the day tomorrow. How's that, Peter?"

"Okay," he said.

Sure, I thought, okay with him, maybe. I was tired now. I didn't care about tomorrow.

I just wanted to swim.

"But I want to ride with Bridget tomorrow," Gracey said from their boat. "I can paddle, too."

"Okay," my dad said. "Tomorrow Peter can ride with Anna and you can ride with us."

Gracey smiled at me, and I didn't feel quite so crabby. But I was still hot.

The rest of the way, every time I dipped my paddle in the water, I imagined that it was my arm, dipping in and out of the water, and I imagined how cool I would feel once I was in that water. A couple times, I scooped up water, splashed my face, and dribbled some down my neck. It was torture to be on the water, not in it, when the sun was so hot.

The wind was very strong coming across the lake, and my arms were achy. The spots behind my armpits burned. My back hurt a little, too.

Soon, Dad started steering the boat closer to shore, and then not much further on I spotted a lean-to on the shore.

"Hey, Dad, I don't see anyone there!" I hollered. It seemed like the wind took my words and just tossed them all over the lake like loose Scrabble letters.

"What?" he said.

I turned around and repeated what I'd just said.

"That's good news!" he shouted.

That's for sure. I did not want to have to unpack a tent tonight. I just wanted to roll out my sleeping bag on the floor of the lean-to and go to sleep.

"Hey, guys, what do you say we race to the lean-to?" Anna shouted from their canoe.

Well, I was tired, but not that tired that I'd give up a chance to race these guys.

"You're on!" I said.

My dad shouted, "Ready, set, go!" and we all dug our paddles in hard. Peter and Gracey were laughing because sitting in the middle of each boat, they were getting splashed and it felt cool. I dug in harder. Our canoe was ahead a little bit.

"Come on Bridget!" my dad yelled.

"Come on Anna!" her dad yelled. "The losers have to make dinner tonight!"

I never paddled so hard before. Their boat pulled ahead, and I dug deeper. We beat them to shore by just a few seconds, and when I heard the belly of our canoe scrape the sandy bottom I thought it was a great sound. We'd landed, and we'd won.

Everyone lugged the canoes on shore and we unloaded what we had to. My legs felt a little wobbly after sitting in a boat all day. I unrolled my sleeping bag next to Anna's in the lean-to, and Gracey unrolled hers on the other side of mine. Then Peter was next to her. The two dads set up in the other lean-to right next to ours.

"Okay, everybody, let's go in the woods for ten minutes and get firewood, and then you guys can swim while I cook," Anna's dad said. "I'll make dinner as head of the losing boat."

"Yahoo!" Peter shouted. "I'm so starving. I could eat a roasted tree with ketchup!"

We all laughed, and went into the woods to find firewood on the forest floor. Ming was happy to be out of the boat and she scampered back and forth, wagging her tail, sniffing every bush and rock. We found little sticks for tinder and some small, dead branches for kindling. That would start the fire. Then we got some logs that would keep the fire going. Each time we found wood, we'd load up our arms, bring it to the front of the lean-to and dump it near the stone fireplace, and then go get more.

Anna's dad was digging a trench in the dirt around the fireplace with a collapsible shovel he'd brought along. A trench would help contain the fire just to the fireplace. We had to be extra careful in the woods so that we didn't start a forest fire.

By the time I returned with my last load, which was two logs, sweat was trickling down my face and from my eyebrows into my eyes. I dropped the logs, and when I looked down at my t-shirt to brush off the dirt from the wood there were two huge spiders crawling on my shirt. They must have been on the log. I screamed and ran into the water! I didn't really even think about anything else except that I was hot and I'd been hot all day and now there were daddy long-leg spiders crawling on me and I didn't want to touch them to brush them off. I just wanted them off me.

I dove right in and went underwater as deep as I could. When my head came back up into the air, I saw Anna, Gracey, and Peter were on shore laughing at me.

"You are silly," Gracey said. Her face was all dirty. She must have wiped her face with her hands after carrying the wood. "You didn't even put your bathing suit on!"

"That's because there were SPIDERS on me," I said. "From the wood. You guys probably have them on you, too."

The three of them screamed and ran into the water, without even looking to see if they had spiders! Then we were all laughing at ourselves and pretty soon Peter was spitting water at Gracey, and Anna was getting

her t-shirt to bubble up with air. I swam underwater and grabbed Peter's legs and we were all just crazy in the wonderful coolness of the lake.

After a while, I swam away from them for a few minutes and just floated on my back and let my tired arms rest. I love looking up at the clouds and the blue, blue sky. I love feeling like the lake is my waterbed. My mom said maybe next year I could get a waterbed at home. I think it will be like floating in a lake all the time.

"Supper's almost ready!" my dad hollered. "Come get into dry clothes, you guys."

I got some dry pants out of my backpack, and a clean t-shirt. When I was pulling them out, I found a letter I had stuffed in my pack at the last minute today. It had arrived in the mail this morning, just as my dad pulled up. He'd wanted me to start loading the truck so I just stuffed it in my pack to read later.

I went off by myself in back of the lean-to for some privacy and sat on a stump. The letter was from my pen pal, Jasmine. She's from Cape Cod. I met her there one year when I went on vacation with my mom. She taught me how to swim in the ocean, and we played at the beach a couple of times that week.

> *Dear Bridget,*
>
> *I hope you're having a great summer. I got a new speed racing bathing suit and I just love it. It's midnight neon blue. Are you coming to the ocean this year? My mom said I could have you for an overnight if you do, or we could have you and your mom over for a cookout. I hope you come. I got two babysitting jobs so far this summer. Both of them were on Friday nights. I made $15 each night. The kids are really cute and I hope they call me again.*

I'm going to crafts camp for a week. What are you doing this summer? Write back soon.
Okay?

> *AFA (A Friend Always)*
> *Jasmine*

I sat on the stump and bit my fingernail. Jasmine has a racer's bathing suit. I can't believe it. That's exactly what I wanted! And it's midnight blue. Oh, boy, and here I'm stuck with this ruffled suit and it's PALE blue. More like baby blue. Midnight blue was so much cooler. Oh, I could never go see Jasmine in my goofy bathing suit. And she's got a babysitting job now! I had just taken the babysitting course and I hadn't gotten a job yet. How could I ever write back to her?

But I wanted to, especially now that she's invited us to see her when I go to the Cape with Mom in August. And I certainly could write to her about this canoe trip. I just wouldn't mention my bathing suit. I would have to convince my mother to get me a new one before we went to Cape Cod. That was just all there was to it.

"Bridget!" my father yelled. "Where are you? We're eating!"

It was starting to get dark, and I came around the corner of the lean-to and found everyone sitting at the picnic table already eating. We had burritos with hamburger, beans, lettuce, and sauce. The dads had made them up ahead of time, so all they had to do was wrap them in foil and heat them at the edge of the fire. They were really good.

Just as we were finishing dinner, we saw a canoe heading toward us. We watched as it came closer, and my dad hollered out "Hello, there!"

The canoe came to shore, and a mom, dad, and girl got out. My dad went to greet them.

"My name's Jim," the dad said, "and this is my wife Susie and our daughter Danielle. This is our first time paddling Long Lake and well, it's taking a lot longer than we thought. I figured we'd be at the end of the lake by tonight, but it's getting dark fast. I was wondering if we could put our tent up at this site, but I don't want to crowd your campsite here . . . "

"Why, sure," my dad said. "You're more than welcome. There's room for all of us."

I looked at Anna. We shrugged, and then stood up and shouted hello to them from our picnic table.

They waved back. "Hi," the dad called to us. "I'm Mr. Jenson, this is Mrs. Jenson, and this is our daughter, Danielle." We hollered out our names.

"We're not from this area," we heard Mr. Jenson say to my dad, "so this is new territory for us. We're from just outside New York City, and we sure do love this chance to get up to the Adirondacks."

"New York City?" Peter whispered to the rest of us. "They're tourists! I bet you they're afraid of bears!"

Anna looked at him and laughed.

"Oh, yeah, and you're afraid of spiders, so don't talk!" she said. "You screamed and jumped in the water and you didn't even know if you had any on you!"

"Oh, I was just jumping in the water because you guys were," Peter said.

Yeah, right, I thought. Just then, I remembered what my dad had said about the "Tourist Information" sign. Suddenly, I had an idea. While the two dads helped the newcomers unload their canoe, I told the others about the sign and how Dad said that "Tourist Information" was information about tourists.

"We have a mission tonight," I said, whispering. "Each of us has to find out something about them that nobody else in our group knows about. They're tourists, and we need information! Then, tomorrow night at our campfire, we'll share the information. Whoever comes up with the best piece of tourist information gets to have my gummy fish candy."

"And my cotton candy bubble gum," Anna said, pulling out a stash from her sweatshirt pocket.

"Oh, goody," Gracey said.

"We have to talk to all of them," I said. "Not just the girl."

We put our hands together on the table, on top of each other's hands in layers, and then pushed our hands up in the air, like a clump of leaves picked up by a breeze. It was our way of saying we agreed not to talk to anyone but each other about our mission.

Chapter 6

The Lost Channel Creature

That night we had so much fun. The campfire had burned down to coals, and it was just perfect for roasting marshmallows. We needed them to make the somemores. Danielle had never had them before. She is eleven years old. Gracey was in charge of the chocolate, of course, and we all cooked our own marshmallows on sticks. Peter kept burning his, but he said he liked them burnt. We put the roasted marshmallows over a piece of chocolate, which was on a graham cracker. Then we put another graham cracker on top and squished it so that the marshmallow melted the chocolate. Peter ate three of them! Danielle said it was the best thing she ever ate. We told her she could sleep in the lean-to with us.

"That's great!" she said. Then she asked to hold Ming. She said her parents didn't want to get a dog because they lived in an apartment in a big city, and they both worked, so they didn't want a dog to be trapped inside all day.

She hugged Ming, and the dog kissed her by licking her cheek.

"Oh, she's a great dog," she said. "Someday I want to have a place with a yard so we can have a pet just like Ming."

Sitting by the fire, Danielle's hair seemed to shine. She has long, shiny blonde hair. I think it's pretty. My hair is dark blonde. This girl at school, who always wears the most expensive clothes and jewelry, told me that my color hair is called dirty blonde. She said she read about hair colors in a fashion magazine her mother had, and mine was definitely dirty blonde. It made me feel awful. I went home and washed my hair three times and sat out in the sun, hoping it would get lighter. It didn't. Jasmine, my pen pal, has auburn hair and a lot of freckles. I wish I had auburn hair like hers because it sparkles in the sun.

Before we did our stories and skits around the campfire, Anna and I helped Danielle roll out her sleeping bag in the lean-to. I held the flashlight so she could see where to put her bag and her little backpack with her clothes in it.

"Have you ever been camping before?" I asked.

"Well, last summer I went to a sleep-away camp, but we had cabins and counselors and everything," she said. "And regular electric lights. I've never been in the woods like this before. My dad said he used to go camping a lot when he was younger, and he wants me to know what it's like. We've gone on a few canoe trips together, but this is our first overnight."

"Do you like being out in the woods?" Anna asked.

"Yeah," Danielle said, smiling. "You know, I really like the city. There's a lot to do, like going to the zoo and the theater, and my ballet class, and Central Park is fun for roller blading. But this is special. I like the woods. Actually, though, I've never ever seen this much dark before in my life!"

Anna and I started laughing. Danielle looked at us as if she didn't understand why we were laughing.

"How can you see the dark?" I asked.

Danielle smiled again. "Well, you know what I mean! Or maybe you don't, because in the city, it's kind of bright even at night because there are so many lights. You never see the sky this dark. And you definitely don't see this many stars. No way."

"Have you ever sat around a campfire?" Anna asked.

"We did at sleep-away camp," Danielle said.

"Well, we're going to do skits," I said, "I hope you like them. Or, you can count the stars while we do our stuff, and tell us how many are out tonight when we're all done! Then you can tell all your friends back home just how many stars there are up in the mountains."

I think Danielle really liked our performances. Peter put the flashlight under his face and it made his face look scary, as if it were long and had dark hollows in it, and it was twitching. He did crazy dances around the campfire, keeping the light on his face and laughing in a low, deep voice. It was a good act. Then Anna and I put on baseball caps and sweatshirts from our fathers' packs and pretended we were dads lost in the woods. We tripped over logs and pretended to fall, and pulled out pieces of paper to make believe we were looking at maps with the wrong directions on them. Our fathers laughed really hard.

Then Gracey put Ming on her leash. First, she pretended she was an old lady walking her dog, and she hunched her back, used a long stick for a cane, and talked in a quivering voice to her little pooch. Then she did a rich lady skit. She put a rolled-up sweatshirt around her neck like a fur collar, and made her dad's fishing cap look like a fancy hat by sticking bird feathers in it and wrapping a vine around it. She put her nose up in the air and walked like a rich, snooty lady who was out walking her pedigreed dog. Ming pranced behind her. "Stay on the other side of the street, please," she said, casting a glance at the rest of us. "I am walking my dog and we do not wish to get soiled by others passing by!"

Finally, for her last act, she pretended she was a colonel in the army walking his dog. "Atten-SHUN!" she said. "March!" and she strutted around the campfire, marching with Ming. She held a stick under her armpit like a baton. She made us all stand up and get inspected.

She does very good impressions. We all laughed a lot.

Anna and Gracey's dad told us some jokes, and then my dad told a ghost story. It was about the ghost of this hermit called Noah John Rondeau, a short, little man with a long beard who had lived by himself in the Adirondacks for years and years all alone in a small cabin on the shores of the Cold River, which branches off the Raquette River not far from here. In order to get to his tiny hut, my father said you had to go past the Dismal Swamp, Bellyache Swamp, and Holy Lost Marsh.

"Old Noah John started out taking people back in there during hunting season, showing them where to hunt," my dad said. "But then he gave up being a guide and he just stayed at Cold River as a hermit. He trapped, hunted, and fished for his food, and that's how he lived. He also

had a little garden. He'd come out of the woods about once a year and buy some canned food and flour, and stuff. He built fires to cook his food."

My father stirred a stick in the fire, sending up sparks. I felt a shiver go up my back.

"He was originally from Canada," he said. "When he first came to America he could only speak French. Later, when he was a hermit and spent all that time alone, he made up his own language using little code drawings."

My dad said the hermit's ghost circled above the trees during the day and came down to the shoreline at night.

"Some folks say when you hear a strange rustle in the woods and you can't spot any animal, or when you hear a splash near the shoreline but you can't see any fish jumping or mink swimming, why it's just Noah John's ghost poking around," my dad said in a loud whisper. "He lived here so long he's like part of the forest. He's a good ghost, though, and he just wants to make sure people are taking care of this part of the Adirondacks."

Still, I mean, he was a ghost, right? We got kind of quiet after that.

I had to go the bathroom right then, but I didn't like leaving the campfire. Even with a flashlight, it suddenly seemed very, very dark. I heard an owl. I moved closer to Anna on our log seat. Some sparks from the fire flew up into the air, and I followed them with my eyes. The trees looked very high and there were a lot of them. They were almost all evergreens. I could see the spires of the balsam trees high up in tight little circles of green. The spruce trees and the Douglas firs I could tell even from here, because they have pine cones. White pine trees are easy to tell because there are five needles in every bundle on the branches, and there's five letters in the word w-h-i-t-e.

It seemed like all the trees were guarding us. We were out in the woods, just our little group, away from any other people and traffic, TV, and telephones. It was just us, and it was dark and quiet. I felt safe when I was around everybody, and I didn't want to move away from the fire. I really loved being here in the woods. Sitting around the campfire in a circle was like all of us being in a little nighttime nest together.

I thought of other things so I wouldn't keep thinking about the ghost story. During the night, I had seen Peter, Gracey, and Anna talking at different times to Mr. and Mrs. Jenson and Danielle. I knew they were getting tourist information. I had been able to talk to the mother and father, but I didn't get any really good information, except that the mother loved coconut and thought it would taste good on somemores, and also that the father snored. I found that out because he told me he hoped he didn't keep us all up with his snoring. Oh, brother, I thought. If that were true, by morning that wouldn't be a secret just for me to share. Everyone would know he snored.

I hadn't talked to Danielle alone yet.

I asked her if she wanted to go to the bathroom before bed with me, but then Anna and Gracey wanted to come, too. So there was no chance to be alone. We all got out our flashlights and went behind the trees. Before we went to bed, my father got out his special canoe map and his flashlight to show Mr. Jenson the canoe route of Long Lake to the

Raquette River. My father had maps for everything.

"When you get to the end of the lake, you're going to head onto the Raquette, as you know. Legend has it that the name, 'Raquette River,' is from a Mohawk Indian name meaning 'Noisy River.' You won't really see why until you get to the falls because up until then it's a peaceful river," my dad said. "But you can really hear the falls. They roar."

My dad has paddled this trip many times. Every year he enters a three-day canoe race from Long Lake to Tupper Lake.

"Just after you get onto the Raquette, you'll see one outlet here off to the right and that can be confusing," he told Mr. Jenson. "So you want to stay left, because you don't want to go up that outlet. It's called The Lost Channel. That leads up to the Cold River, where Noah John Rondeau used to live."

I looked at Anna across the campfire and she was looking at me. Her eyes were wide. I knew we were both thinking the same thing. The Lost Channel? What did that mean?

"Okay, guys, time for bed," my dad said. He went down to the lake, filled our bucket with water, and began putting out the fire. It sizzled when the water hit the coals, and thick smoke filled the air. He filled the bucket with water many times to be sure the fire was out, and filled the trench with water.

"I don't like that smell," Gracey said. "I'm getting in my sleeping bag and covering up."

"Clean up first," her dad said, and he filled a bucket with water and brought it behind the lean-to for us to wash up. He said we should never wash with soap in the lake because too much soap, toothpaste, and shampoo can harm a lake or river. We should always wash up well away from the lake, the same with going to the bathroom, so we don't pollute the water.

Gracey's face was covered with marshmallow goo. I told her she looked like a ghost with all that white sticky stuff.

That was the wrong thing to say.

"I don't want any ghosts to think I'm a ghost," she said, looking like she was going to cry. "Then they'll want to come talk to me. I don't want that hermit to take me off into the woods."

I sure didn't want Gracey to cry because she cries really loud. I helped her wash her face so she didn't look like a ghost, and promised her I'd sleep very close to her.

We all got in the lean-to. I made sure my flashlight was in the sleeping bag with me, along with Lester, the teddy bear my dad gave me when he and my mom got divorced.

"Can I sleep with Ming?" Danielle asked. "I love your dog." I told her she could.

I told Gracey two bedtime stories before she fell asleep. Then I rolled over to talk to Danielle. Now, finally, I could get some tourist information none of the others had. She had squeezed her bag right next to mine, and now we could talk, just the two of us.

"Danielle!" I whispered.

There was no answer. I leaned closer to her to see if she was awake. Her eyes were shut, but her mouth was open, and a little, gravely sound was coming out of it. Then I realized—she was snoring! It wasn't a loud snore, but it was a snore for sure. Oh, great! She must take after her father.

"Anna!" I said, turning the other way and looking over Gracey's head. "Are you awake?"

"Yes," she said. "I'm thinking about the Lost Channel. Why do you think it's named that? I mean, who got lost in there?"

"I don't know," I said. "Maybe it's filled with the bodies of dead people who got lost and could never find their way back out. Wouldn't that be awful?"

"Or worse, maybe there's a Lost Channel creature. People who take their canoes down there never come back alive because the creature captures them," Anna said.

"Yeah, and the creature puts the people in an underwater cave, with just their heads sticking out," Peter piped up from the other end of the lean-to, suddenly very wide-awake. "And they don't have any food or water and just their heads are sticking out in the hot sun and they gasp and beg to be set free, but the Lost Channel creature just laughs really loud. He can't talk; he only makes grunting noises or weird laughing noises."

He made some noises in his throat to show what he meant. We all laughed.

Then he went on: "Maybe he's the ghost of Noah John Rondeau, and after all those years of being quiet by himself, he wants to be loud! But he forgot how to talk because he was alone for so long, so he can only grunt. And he's not really mean, but he wants some company and he

doesn't want people to leave!"

"He could have a long, slimy beard like Noah and you can see his bones through his skin," Anna joined in. "His bones look like piles of little fish bones because he ate so much fish while he was a hermit!"

"Yeah," I said, sitting up, "and after he captures the people and they are his prisoners, the loons swim by and make laughing noises. They're crazy loons that live only in the Lost Channel." Loons are beautiful black and white birds we often see on quiet Adirondack lakes. They make wonderful chortling noises way out on the lake. It sounds kind of haunting. We always try to imitate them, but it's a hard noise to make. Loons can also go underwater for a long time.

"Or maybe the Lost Channel creature goes underwater and tickles the feet of the people so hard that after awhile they go crazy and start laughing like loons and they can't get away," Anna said. She hates to have her feet tickled.

"And then, finally, the trapped people just wither and die in the cold, damp cave," Peter said, hanging his head as if he was one of the captured people about to die.

"I hope we don't ever end up in the Lost Channel," I said.

"Me neither," Anna and Peter said at the same time.

We added some more details about the creature, like his beard was probably filled with dead minnows and weeds. We were so tired we could barely talk after awhile, and first Peter fell asleep and then Anna, and then I was awake all by myself. I didn't want to close my eyes. I was very, very tired from all the paddling, but I wanted to look out at the stars I could see above the lake from the inside of the lean-to. I didn't want to fall asleep thinking about whether or not there really was a Lost Channel creature. It seemed funny when all three of us were talking about it, but now that I was the only one awake, it seemed more real, and scary.

Finally, I drifted off to sleep, only to be woken up some time later by a strange, loud noise I could hear every few seconds. I thought at first of the creature, and how Peter said it might make grunting noises. Whatever else could that noise be but Rondeau wanting some company in the Lost Channel? He might be lonely for years to come. It certainly wasn't a loon.

Carefully, I pulled my flashlight out and turned it on. I shone it over all the kids. Everyone was sleeping and quiet. Ming was curled up close to Danielle. I didn't dare leave the lean-to, but I crawled to the edge and flashed the light out over the water. I couldn't hear anything. I looked for ripples in the water, just in case . . .

At the edge of the lean-to, the noise was even louder, and I could tell it was coming from the right. I shone the light over. It landed on Danielle's parents tent, where the noise was very loud. It was snoring! It was her father's snoring. I have never heard such loud snoring in my whole life. The sides of the tent moved in and out. I couldn't believe it!

Finally, I fell back asleep. I dreamt about ghosts that snored.

I woke up to the smell of pancakes my dad was making in a cast iron frying pan set on top of the grill over the fireplace. He already had a fire going by the time we got up.

I was a little bit tired and sore, but I was happy to wake up to

50

friends and food. I rolled over to say hello to Ming. And the next thing you know I was hollering "Oh, no!"

Ming had gotten into Anna's bubble gum, and she had big gobs of chewed pink gum covering her hair. Now she was black and white and pink. She even had a big wad of gum stuck on her upper lip.

"Ming!" I said. "What did you do? You're a bad dog!"

She put her head down on the floor of the lean-to between her paws. She always does that when she knows she's been bad. Carefully, she looked up at me, keeping her head on the floor, to see what I was going to do. I think she knows how cute she looks when she does that.

Just then, Peter woke up, took one look at Ming, and couldn't stop laughing, and then Gracey did the same. She really did look comical. The gobs hung off her like Christmas tree ornaments or mushy Easter eggs. When she heard everybody laughing, she jumped up and started wagging her tail. She thought she was funny now.

I told her to lie down. Then I took out my pocketknife, and carefully cut all the gum out of her hair. I took her to the lake, and used the water to get the gum off her lip. She wasn't very happy and kept whining when I had to pull on her lip. It must have hurt. I talked to her in a soft voice while I was doing it to keep her calm.

Danielle and her parents didn't stay for breakfast; they said they wanted to get an early start because they were slow paddlers and they wanted to get to the falls so they could relax and fish. We waved good-bye. Danielle gave Ming a long hug.

I felt disappointed I didn't have any information about Danielle. I liked her, and it would have been nice to get to know her better. Maybe we'd see them at the falls. I sure wished I had some information for our tourist contest.

I ate a lot of pancakes that morning. I put jam on some of them and real maple syrup on others. After breakfast, I was rolling up my sleeping bag to begin loading the canoe when I saw something shiny underneath my bag. The sun was hitting it and it was glinting. I thought maybe Ming's dog tag had fallen off. I picked it up. It was a silver bracelet and it had red writing on it.

It said "Medic Alert."

On the back, it said "Danielle Jenson. Diabetic."

My eyes got big. Wow. Danielle had diabetes. That must be scary. I knew that people with diabetes have problems with the sugar level in their body, and some diabetics have to take something called insulin or they can get very sick. Usually they have to have shots of insulin, or sometimes, if they haven't eaten they get weak and they have to get something to eat or drink right away to raise their sugar level. I know this because a kid in my class is diabetic and one time she did a report in school on it. She said she hated going to birthday parties because she could never eat cake because she wasn't allowed to have sugar.

I'd have to be sure and get this bracelet back to Danielle. Maybe we'd meet up with them later at the falls. But for now, boy did I ever have the best piece of tourist information! And nobody else but me knew about it! Wait until I told the others at the campfire tonight.

Today was going to be an exciting day. I just knew it. I was sure to win the tourist information contest, and not only that, but tonight, Anna and I were going to do our secret ceremony at the falls that we'd been waiting to do for so long.

I could hardly get in the canoe fast enough.

Chapter Seven

Flying in the Water

By the time we got to the river, we were thrilled to be paddling on peaceful water and to be out of the wind. It was like entering another world to come off a big wide lake into a river with the banks close by on either side and rich, green hemlock and cedar trees hanging over the banks. The current was steady, so we didn't have to paddle as hard, either. Our fathers let us pull to shore after awhile, and we got out of the canoes and jumped in the water. Then we swam alongside the canoes while the fathers drifted along in the boats, paddling a bit. I swam in another pair of shorts and t-shirt that I had.

In some places, when we dangled our legs down, we could feel cool spots in the water.

When my dad said we were coming up to the entrance to the Lost Channel, I told him I wanted to get back in the boat. I didn't want to take a chance on old, bony Noah John Rondeau grabbing onto my legs with his ghost hands, or sliming me with his ghost beard, probably smelling like swamp water by now. No thank you. Peter, Gracey, and Anna all suddenly wanted to get back in the canoes, too.

We all got back into the boats, and began paddling again. My dad told us the Raquette River is the second longest river in New York State after the Hudson. Even though it starts pretty close to the Hudson River, they flow in different directions. The Raquette travels north, the same direction we are going.

I knew we were almost to the carry when I saw the sign that said Dangerous Falls Ahead. Soon we'd have to get out and carry our canoes around the waterfalls.

Pointing to the sign with his paddle, my dad said, "Hey, we better enjoy summer while we can because we're going to have to be on guard the next couple of autumn seasons. There's dangerous falls ahead!"

We all splashed him with our paddles, and even Anna's dad told him that was his silliest sign story yet.

Once we got to the carry, we had to unload each boat and carry a lot of gear. I put my backpack on, and carried a plastic bag with my sleeping bag in it and another backpack with food. The others took their backpacks, and Anna had a big sack with the flashlights and pots and dishes in it. Ming walked ahead of me. Our fathers carried one canoe. They flipped it over and carried it on their shoulders. They would come back and get the other canoe.

The carry, which is also called a portage, was worse than dreadful. The trail was rocky, the mosquitoes were biting me, and worst of all, we couldn't even see the falls from the trail. My dad said once we reached the end of the trail, we would set up camp near the falls. Then we could actually walk to the falls from another path called the lower trail. It went alongside both the upper and lower falls.

"Hey, Dad, is an upper fall when just the top of your body falls over?" I asked.

"Yeah, and a lower fall is when you hit your knee and you fall from the bottom part of your body!" Anna joined in from behind me. We all laughed.

It was good to get a break from thinking about how hot and grumpy I felt. This was the only part of the trip I didn't really like so far, even though it did feel good to stretch my legs after being in the canoe so much. I smacked another mosquito; this one bit me on the neck. I scratched the spot right away.

I was so, so glad when we finally got to the lean-to.

"Ugh," I said, sitting down on my backpack. "Finally!"

"Hey, sport, just think, at least you don't have to go back. We do!" my father said.

"Would you like something to drink, first?" I asked.

He smiled. "Sure."

I got him out a juice box. I was glad I remembered that I wasn't the only one who was hot and tired. At least I didn't have to carry a boat!

He pointed down the trail a bit from the lean-to. "Walk a bit that way," he said, "and to the right you'll find the edge of the meadow. That's where you and Anna can set up your tent. You'll see a ranger's cabin not too far away. You'll love being in the meadow. The whole place lights up at night with fireflies," he said.

"I can't wait," I said. "And it's not too far from the lean-to where the rest of you are sleeping, is it?"

"No," he said. "Don't worry. And when we get back from bringing the second canoe, we'll pile up some big wood so you girls can have your own campfire."

So Anna and I set off for the meadow, taking Peter and Gracey with us. We could already hear the falls. We found a good spot and put up our tent. It didn't take long. It was just a little pup tent. Ming got inside as soon as we had it up and sniffed around.

"Hey," Gracey said. "It's a pup tent for a puppy!"

"Yeah," I said. "Now, I think we should all get some wood for our tent and for the lean-to. Let's surprise our fathers and get the wood, because they're going to be really tired going back across that carry again."

"I'm too tired," Peter said.

"Wouldn't you rather get it now," Anna said, "and then we can swim and cool off? Once we're swimming, you're not going to want to go get wood."

"Okay," Peter said reluctantly.

So, we all got piles of branches and kindling and dragged a few logs out of the woods. Our dads could chop them up with the axe. By the time we were done, we were hot and dirty. Everyone except me changed into swimsuits and then sat down in the grass to wait for our fathers. I put on my last pair of dry shorts and another t-shirt.

Just then, we heard the screen door of the ranger's cabin bang shut. I turned around. The cabin was beautiful. It was made of logs and had a big screened-porch. I thought how nice it must be to live there and hear the waterfalls every day and every night.

"How do you do? I'm the ranger here, and my name is Michael," he said, shaking our hands. We introduced ourselves.

"You guys look awful hot," he said. "Where are your folks?"

"Right here!" we heard behind us, and turned to see our dads coming out of the trail.

They both shook hands with the ranger and introduced themselves.

"You look even hotter than the kids!" Ranger Michael said.

"Well, we just made our second trip on the carry," my dad said. "We had two canoes."

"How would you all like to go swimming in the chute?" Ranger Michael said. "I have to practice my rescue throws, and I could practice with you guys."

"What's a chute?" Gracey asked.

"Well, it's a stream of water that's still moving very fast from just coming over the falls," the ranger said. "If you guys swim out into the chute, I'll throw out my rescue rope and drag you back upstream. I need some practice."

Peter's eyes lit up. "Wow," he said. "That sounds great."

We raced down the path to the water at a spot below the lower falls. Following the ranger, we waded out to a rock, and then two by two, we jumped into the water off the other side of the rock. The river was cool and fast. The fast-moving current quickly swept us away from the rock and down the river. All we had to do was be still, and the water zoomed us

along. We screamed and laughed as it carried us past everything on shore.

I jumped in with Gracey, holding her hand. The current was so fast that it felt like we were flying through the water. Then, just as it seemed as if we were going to be carried away from everyone and never get back, Gracey hollered "Save us Ranger Mike!" He took the rope out of his rescue bag and flung one end of it over to us. It arced high above the water and then splashed down right next to us. I grabbed it, and then Gracey, holding onto me, grabbed it too. Ranger Mike pulled us back to the rock, and it was a blast because we could feel the pull of the water one way from the current going downstream, and the pull of the water against us as he hauled us back to the rock.

We took turns and jumped off the rock again and again, flying down the river before we got rescued. We swam until we were so tired we could hardly hold onto the rope anymore. Then it was time for a break. It was the best time I ever had in the water.

We headed back up the path to change and make dinner, and soon, Anna and I told each other, it would be time to have our secret ceremony at the campfire.

Chapter Eight

The Secret Ceremony

We walked back up the trail together and went right to the lean-to where our dads had left the canoes. We put on sweatshirts because it was cooling down and the mosquitoes were out.

Just as we got the fire going, Willie, Charlie, and their older cousin Jamie came walking up the trail.

"Hello, guys, we were wondering when you'd get here!" my dad shouted. "You're just in time for dinner."

"Good," said Charlie, "I love to eat and we didn't catch any fish today."

"Have you been here awhile?" Anna's dad asked.

"We rode in on our horses a couple of hours ago," Jamie said. "We've been fishing at the lower falls."

"Well, we've got plenty of food," my dad said. "Bridget, why don't you see if Ranger Michael would like to join us for dinner."

Anna and I raced off to the cabin to get the ranger. He said he'd love to join us. On the way to the lean-to, I asked him if he'd seen a mother, father, and girl with long blonde hair today.

"Oh, yeah," he said. "They said they were going to hike up to the upper falls and fish and read all day. I think they set up their tent off the trail over that way." He pointed to his left.

"Oh, good, then we'll see them tomorrow I hope," I said. "If you see them first, make sure you tell them we're here. I have something that belongs to the girl. Her name's Danielle."

"What do you have?" Anna asked.

"I can't tell yet," I whispered to her. "It's part of our tourist information mission. Since we're going to see them tomorrow, we'll have another chance to get more information, so I don't want to tell tonight."

That night we cooked hot dogs on sticks and my dad heated up some beans in a cooking pan. He also put some corn on the cob in the coals after wrapping them in aluminum foil, and we had those to eat, too.

We told Willie, Charlie, and Jamie all about our adventures swimming in the chute, and how much fun it was. They hadn't even been swimming yet because they'd been fishing.

"Where are your horses?" I asked.

"They're tied up way in back of the meadow, where the foot trail ends," Jamie said. "They'll be all right for awhile. I'll go roll out my sleeping bag later and sleep near them. I like sleeping outdoors anyway."

I made sure Ming got a good dinner from the food I'd packed for her, and I also gave her a couple of treats of her favorite flavored bones. Then she gave a big sigh and fell sound asleep at my feet. She sure had done a lot of running today.

"Can we make somemores?" Charlie asked before he was done with the last bite of his hot dog. "I'm still hungry."

"Me, too," Peter said. "I'm starving. I've been starving all day."

"Lucky for you, I have chocolate left," Gracey said.

So, we started roasting marshmallows and making somemores. Every time I looked over at Charlie, he was eating another one. His face was covered with marshmallow goo.

"Charlie!" I said. "How many have you had?"

"I think I ate four," he said, giving me a big smile.

"You sure do have a big appetite for a little guy," Ranger Michael said to Charlie.

"I'm not that little," Charlie said. "I'm ten. I'm just short. But I'm a lot taller when I wear my cowboy boots. Do you think tomorrow maybe you can take me to the chute?"

"Maybe," Ranger Michael said with a smile.

"How did you learn how to do that rope trick everyone's talking about?" Willie asked. "Did you ever have to rescue anyone from the water?"

"I sure have," the ranger said. "Once a man got overtired while he was swimming, and he started getting carried away in the current. Another time a boy fell out of his canoe and he couldn't swim. Luckily, I was right there. I'd been working on the dock that day. And once, believe it or not, I had to get rescued here myself. Not from the water, though."

We all looked at him, waiting to hear how that could happen to a ranger.

He lifted the lid of his old green hat and wiped sweat from his head.

"Well, one time I was clearing brush, you know, old dead branches and stuff, off the trail to the lower falls. Sometimes, after a storm, we get what we call 'blow down' and it all has to be cleared away. Well, I needed to rest and I leaned up against a boulder. I didn't realize the boulder was loose, and perched right on a cliff, and when I leaned on it the boulder moved and started rolling. Since I had all my weight on the rock, I lost my balance and fell into a ravine, and the boulder rolled right on top of me!" he said.

We were all sitting there, listening, our eyes as wide as could be.

"I never thought I'd get out of that mess," he said. "I leaned over, got a thick stick and pushed and pried that boulder off me. I was so sweaty and the mosquitoes were biting me everywhere. And I hurt everywhere. The boulder broke my pelvis," he said, pointing to the area around his hips.

"I finally rolled the boulder off, and then I knew I had to crawl up that hill. It took me two hours to crawl out of that ravine and get back on the trail. But I knew if I didn't, no one would ever find me down there. It hurt so bad to crawl I thought my face would never look the same because it was all twisted up in pain," he said.

I looked over, and Charlie was scrunching up his face, just like the ranger was doing as he remembered how much he had ached.

"Finally," Ranger Michael said, "I made it back up to the trail and I just lay there for a long time. I tried to holler every now and then, but I was so weak."

He looked over at Jamie. "Luckily, Jamie's dad, who has lead horseback trips into the falls for years, was on an overnight trip here with his wife. They found me on the trail as they came up to go fishing."

"How did they carry you out if you were all broken?" Charlie asked.

"Well, I told Jamie's dad to go to the old barn near my cabin. There's a bunch of old doors in there from when folks had lodges here at the falls for travelers. They brought back a door, and he and his wife used it like a stretcher. They put me on the door and carried me out of the woods and down to my boat. They had to drive the boat at night, too, dark as could be. The moon was nowhere to be found that night; it was so cloudy," Ranger Mike said. "Luckily, I know the river as well as can be and I know every turn, so I could direct them," he said. "We got to the landing and my truck was there and they loaded me in the back and took me to the hospital. Boy, it was a bumpy ride. I was in the hospital for a couple of weeks."

"Wow," Willie said. "I hope I never mess with a big boulder like that. You're lucky!"

"And we're lucky you're okay because you're still here at the falls, and you helped us have a great day!" Anna said.

"I had fun today, too," he said. "Thanks for dinner. I guess I better be going now. Good-night everyone."

We said good night. We were all too tired to sing songs or do chants, and besides, Anna and I wanted to get to our own little tent just down the trail. We had our secret ceremony to perform.

But just then, I heard a groan and looked over at Charlie. He was holding his stomach. I noticed he had become pretty quiet.

"I think I ate too much," he said.

Suddenly he stood up and ran off in the woods, and then we heard this loud noise like a sick growl. Ugh, Charlie was throwing up. It sounded gross. I held onto my own stomach, hoping it would stay nice and quiet. I hate it when someone vomits in school. It always makes me feel like I'm going to heave, too, especially if I can smell it.

At least Charlie wasn't throwing up near the lean-to.

Willie and Peter just thought it was funny.

"Hey," Willie said, "one time Sparky Jones puked right on the bus and it was all over the seat."

"Yeah, that's nothing," Peter said. "This kid in gym class threw up in his sneaker . . ."

"Okay," my dad said, "that's enough. We've all just eaten."

When Charlie walked back over to the campfire, his face looked pale. My dad took him down to the river to wash his face off and let him cool down a bit.

"Come on, Anna!" I said, standing up. "That's a sure sign that it's time to go."

"Please can I come, too?" Gracey asked. "I don't want to stay here with Charlie. He has puke breath now for sure. Please don't make me stay."

I didn't know what to do. I thought our secret ceremony might scare her, and I didn't want to do that. I looked at Anna and she shrugged.

"I promise I'll go right to sleep in the tent," Gracey said. "I won't sit with you guys out by your fire. I'll just lie down with Ming. Plus, Bridget, back in the canoe, you promised you'd tell me what you guys were whispering about."

She picked up Ming and held her in her arms.

"See?" she said. "We'll cuddle together." She gave us one of her cutest smiles.

Well, I couldn't say no to that. "You're right, Gracey, I did promise. Come along, and we'll all sleep in the tent tonight."

We picked up our flashlights and our backpacks. My dad came with us to help us start a fire. Then he walked down to the lake with us and we each filled up a bucket of water to put the fire out later.

"Now the ranger cabin's right there," he said when we got back to our tent. "Even if the ranger's not there, you could always go on the porch if you get startled or something, and you know we're just a little bit down the trail."

"Okay, Dad," I said. "Good-night."

We watched him walk away, and then Anna and I hugged each other, we were so excited. It was our first night camping without adults.

We told Gracey she could sit by the fire for a little while, and while she did we talked about what an exciting day it had been.

"I think I'm a really fast swimmer now," Gracey said. "Now that I know what it feels like to move so fast in the water, I bet I can swim down that chute all by myself!"

"I think we all better swim together," I said. "That water moves fast. Once we get out on the river again, though, we can all swim alongside the boats, and you don't need to hold onto anyone to do that. You're a good enough swimmer."

"Yeah, I like doing that," Gracey said.

"Okay, come on, you have to go to bed now," Anna said. I knew she wasn't that happy that her little sister had come along tonight. I guess when you have brothers and sisters you get tired of them sometimes.

So Gracey and Ming went in the tent, and we gave her a flashlight of her own and zipped up her sleeping bag. I told Gracey that we were going to do some dancing by the fire, that was all, and make a little ceremony with some music. Ming sniffed the sides of the tent, and then flopped down next to Gracey. She curled up right against her belly.

Outside by the fire, Anna and I took out our feathers from our backpacks.

"I have a red-tail hawk feather and a crow's feather," I said.

"I have a night hawk feather," she said.

We had already decided that we would use an upside down pot for a drum. What we were going to do was an Indian ghost dance. We'd learned about it in school, studying Native Americans. We had learned that some Indians had started doing ghost dances as a way to call back the spirits of their people who had been killed in wars. They always did them around a fire because the light was powerful. We thought if we drummed, like many Indians did in their ceremonies, and laid out the feathers near the fire, it would be like an invitation for the Indian spirits. Native Americans used feathers a lot in their ceremonies. They were very close to nature and especially to birds and animals.

"I've been thinking," Anna said. "Maybe we should try to see if the ghost of Noah John Rondeau would come to the fire—even though he's not Indian. Since we're near to where he lived, and your dad told us all about him, he might come to us."

"It's worth a try," I said, slowly. "But when we talked about doing it for Indians, it didn't seem that scary, because they're used to ceremonies. Somehow, it seems scary to think of doing it for Noah John after all that stuff we made up about him, being the Lost Channel creature and all. Maybe he won't like that very much. I mean, we didn't make up any creature stories about Indians so they wouldn't be upset with us."

"Well," Anna said quite matter-of-factly. "The ghost dance is a way to bring blessings back to the earth, and to the people. So if we see Noah John, we could just tell him everything's still okay here on the Raquette River. Really, if you do see any ghosts, it's supposed to just be a way to visit with them. The Native Americans did it because they lost so many relatives in ugly wars. This was a way for them to see their relatives again and to heal from their sadness."

Anna knows a lot about history. That's the one class where she always gets better grades than I do.

"Well, I'll give it a try," I said.

"Besides," she said, "the ceremony tonight is really for any Indians who hunted and fished in this area long ago and maybe lost their lives to a wild animal or in a fight with another person. We just want to let the hermit know if he's around, that he's welcome, too."

"Okay," I said.

Anna took a stick and started drumming on the pot. I walked around the campfire, holding the feathers up to the sky. Sparks from our fire swirled up in the air, and I followed them with my eye, looking beyond them to the stars. It was so clear here, I felt like I could see every single star in the universe.

After we did that for a while, Anna got out a tape and her portable cassette player. It runs on batteries. She got the tape from the public library. It was a tape of Native Americans chanting.

"Hey, Anna, look," I said, pointing out to the meadow. We could see fireflies everywhere. They were little dots of light flickering in the wildflowers.

"It makes it even more magical," Anna whispered.

"Maybe fireflies are spirits!" I said. "You know, I never thought of that before. Maybe they're spirits that come to light our way in the darkness."

"Gracey says that they're tiny lanterns for the fairies," Anna said. "She says fairies are too small to carry their own lights, so the fireflies light the way for them so they can see at night. That's why the fireflies are always low to the ground, because that's where the fairies are."

"I think my mom must have told her that when you guys slept over before," I said. "Because that's what my mom always told me. She says the fairies have their own houses inside tree trunks, and the fireflies come inside with them late at night and they are their nightlights."

Anna put the tape in. We started chanting along with the music, and dancing around the campfire. At first, we felt a little silly, but the tape just sort of made you want to dance. Music can do that. The Indians chanted, and sometimes they moaned. Drumbeats sounded.

The longer we danced around the fire, the more we couldn't take our eyes off of it. The flames were blue and orange. They seemed to melt and then come back to life. Even though I knew the flames were burning the wood, it seemed as if they were just dancing around each log, just like we were dancing around the fire. The longer I stared into the flame, the more it seemed as if I were kind of dreaming standing up.

Our steps got slower, and after awhile we were just staring into the fire, tired, and kind of swaying back and forth and chanting softly. Even above the music, I could hear the summer breeze ruffle the leaves above and all around us. It was like the wind was singing them a lullaby.

Then I heard another sound. It was like a low groan. I looked over at Anna to see if she heard it. Her eyes were jumping around, looking. She had definitely heard something.

The sparks seemed to be higher all of a sudden. I followed them upward again with my eyes. So did Anna. For just a couple of seconds I thought my heart would stop, because I saw something misty float above the sparks. It wasn't just a shapeless mist, either; it was long and thick, like a person. And it looked like it had a beard.

I couldn't speak. I went over to the other side of the fire to stand closer to Anna. My heart didn't feel like it had stopped anymore, instead it felt like it was pumping water like a fire engine.

Chapter Nine

The Scare

We both heard another moan.

Anna grabbed onto my arm. We were both still looking up.

"Say something!" I whispered to her.

"Aren't the spirits supposed to talk to us?" she asked. "I mean, we don't even know who it is. It could be the ghost of Noah John Rondeau, or the ghost of one of the guides who used to camp here at the falls all the time. Or it could be an Indian who used to hunt here."

So, we just kept looking up. Now it seemed like there were three separate forms of misty smoke. One seemed bigger than the other. I sure hoped it wasn't a Lost Channel creature. I thought maybe I should say something, anything, to show that we were friendly.

Just then, one of the people chanting on the tape moaned really loudly, and I jumped. Now I better say something for sure, so they know it's just Anna and me down here, and not a whole bunch of people who are sick and moaning and might scare them away.

"Hello?" I said.

There was no answer. The sparks flew up into the night sky. Between the sparks and the stars, there were three shapes, and they seemed more solid all the time. I thought for sure I could see a face on one, and a robe on another. I felt goose bumps down my arm.

"Anna," I said, "I think one is an Indian chief."

She nodded her head.

"Hello?" I said again. "Can you talk?"

There was no answer. My neck hurt from looking up, and the fire caught my eye as a flame hit a knot in one of the logs and spit out sparks. Then I noticed something beyond the fire. I nudged Anna, and pointed. Past the flames, reaching into the meadow, I could see shadowy figures. They were much different than the misty shapes above us. These were tall shadows and they were thick. Now the woods seemed to be full of shadows. I felt tingly everywhere, and frozen in place at the same time. Were the spirits slowly moving to earth? What was happening here?

Anna and I held onto each other's arms. I tried to make myself breathe.

The shapes seemed to be moving closer. I felt every hair on the back of my neck stand up.

Finally, I asked again, only my voice was quivering this time, "Hello? We're just a couple of girls camping here. Can you speak to us?"

The shadows seemed to be moving around us. I dug my hands into Anna's arm.

"YES WE CAN!" came a deep voice from behind me, and both Anna and I screamed and ran without looking behind us.

Then we heard it.

The laughing.

The sound of boys laughing.

It was Willie and Charlie. They'd snuck up behind us. We came crashing back through the meadow, hollering at them. I wanted to cry. I mean, I was mad, but I was also jumpy, and I was confused. If they were the shadows, what were the misty shapes? Suddenly I was shivering. I heard Ming barking, and went into the tent to get her and calm her down. Luckily, Gracey was still asleep.

"That was MEAN!" I said when I came back out of the tent, holding Ming.

"You guys are jerks!" Anna said.

I looked back up into the sky above our campfire. There was no sign of any form or shape.

"What were you guys doing, chanting weird stuff around a campfire? You guys are strange," Willie said.

"Yeah," Charlie piped in.

"Shouldn't you be in the sick ward?" I said to Charlie. "You do have vomit breath still, in case you didn't notice."

I stormed into the tent, and came back out with my backpack.

"You guys think you're so tough," I said. "Well, never mind what we were doing. It's part of an ancient, secret ceremony, and if you want to know more, you'll have to pass a test. Anna and I read about it in a book about the Adirondacks. Did you know the name Adirondack means bark-eater? Well, if you want to be a real Adirondacker, a real tough one like you guys THINK you are, well, then you have to prove it by eating bark."

I took some pieces from the front pocket of my backpack. I had picked them up on the trail while we were carrying our stuff to the lean-tos. I'd had this plan ever since we were in the canoes yesterday on Long Lake.

"Here!" I said, thrusting it at them. "Go ahead. I DARE you."

"And if you chicken out," Anna said, "We'll tell EVERYONE that Charlie was such a baby he threw up in the woods because he was so scared to be in the forest and that you guys weren't even brave enough to be bark-eaters like the Indians."

At first, Willie just stared at us like we were crazy. But Charlie tugged at his sleeve.

"Come on, Willie, I don't want them telling everybody I threw up 'cause I was scared."

"Oh," Willie said, "You think I'm afraid to eat bark? I've eaten worse than that. I've eaten worms."

He grabbed the bark from my hand and stuffed it his mouth. I could hear it crunch as he chewed.

Charlie just took a little bite. He was probably afraid to throw up again. He only chewed it with his front teeth, and then spit it out.

Willie opened his mouth when he was done. It was all black. There were little pieces of bark in his teeth.

"I swallowed mine," he said. "So there. Come on Charlie, let's go to bed now. We'll leave these girls to their own weird stuff. We really got them good this time. Ha ha."

Anna and I watched them walk away. Then we put the fire out with the buckets of water, and stomped all around the campfire to make sure there were no more sparks or little pieces of coal that might have fallen out of the fire.

We went in the tent. Gracey was sound asleep. Ming walked around in circles for a while at my feet, trying to calm down from all the excitement.

It was very, very late. So much had happened today. Anna and I fell asleep in seconds. We barely said goodnight to each other. I fell asleep and had dreams about Indian songs, and a group of fairies who had tiny campfires every night. They didn't need matches to start the fires because the fireflies lit them.

And then I dreamt about shapes in the mist, and it was a peaceful dream.

Chapter Ten

The Waddling Walrus

The next day we all wanted to hike the trail to the lower and upper waterfalls. Both of our dads wanted to fish near the lower falls, and then they said we could all swim later.

Since all of my shorts were still wet from the swimming I'd been doing, I went in the tent and put on my ruffled bathing suit, and then just put a t-shirt over it that I would wear while we were walking. Then I could just peel off the t-shirt and jump in the water when it was time to swim. That way, no one would see me in that ugly bathing suit. I put on my socks and sneakers, and stuffed my small daypack with a couple of towels, along with some juice boxes, apples, and, of course, candy. I hung my wet shorts over some low tree branches so they could dry in the sun. I'd need a pair for tomorrow, our last day of paddling.

Gracey said she liked my bathing suit. I gave her a hug, and held out my hand to walk with her. I called Ming, and we all started walking with Anna, Peter, and our dads. Willie and Charlie were already at the falls with their cousin Jamie, fishing. They'd left early.

The trail to the falls was a beautiful, woodsy path. The forest floor was covered with pine needles, and the air was filled with the smell of balsam. We could hear the falls while we walked, and we couldn't wait to see them. First, we came to the lower falls. They're not high, like a long, thin tumbling waterfall, but they're really wide and very powerful. The water looks thick and strong and it's crystal clear as it rushes over the rocks. At one end, a bend where the rocks jutted out made a space for the water just like a bubbling whirlpool.

Our dads said we could just relax there for a while and have lunch while they fished, and then we'd go swimming later. They had packed us some peanut butter and jam sandwiches.

First, though, we walked around on the rocks near the falls. There were pools of water between the rocks, and some of them had tiny minnows in them, or water bugs swimming along the top. I saw two beautiful dragonflies together and they were as blue as the sky.

It was hot walking around in the sun, and finally I took my t-shirt off so I could cool off and so I'd have something to sit on while we ate. Peter caught a little frog in one of the pools, and he held it up proudly while it wiggled in his hand, its legs dangling down.

"I'm going to name it Crazy Legs," he said. "I'm going to bring it home in the canoe and keep it in my room."

"You better ask my dad first," Anna said. "I don't think it'd be good for a frog to spend tonight in a bucket, and then be in a canoe in the hot sun all day tomorrow."

Peter frowned. "I want this frog," he said. "I'll go ask. And I'm going to stay over there and fish for a while, too."

So, off he went to fish with our dads, who were just a little way down from the falls. Sometimes I like to fish, but today all I wanted to do was sit and relax. I took off my sneakers and socks, and put them in my pack.

"I'm so tired from yesterday," I told Anna as we sat and ate. "First we paddled all day and then we did all that dancing. I'm glad we're not paddling anywhere today. Wasn't it weird being around the fire? Everything seemed so different."

"Yeah," Anna said. "Too bad Willie and Charlie came along. I mean, it seems like a dream, now that it's daylight and the whole night is over. But I think something was going on at our campfire and up in that sky."

"I saw you guys for a while," Gracey said, "before I fell asleep. I think you're good dancers. And Anna, I won't tell Mommy you were up so late."

"Thanks," Anna said. She looked over Gracey's head at me and smiled. We were both so glad Gracey hadn't woken up when we screamed at the shadows and at Willie and Charlie's voices. She would have been scared all night.

"Are there any cookies left?" Gracey asked. I bent over the little insulated pack my father had brought to see if there were any left.

"Oh, look at this," I heard behind me. "What is this creature with ruffles?"

I turned around and saw Willie and Charlie standing there, smiling at me. That's when I remembered I had on my bathing suit, with the ruffles. I could feel my face get red.

Willie had a fishing pole in one hand, and he slapped the side of his leg with his other hand.

"Well," he said, "if it's not a BABY BLUE WALRUS getting ready for a swim."

"Yeah," Charlie said, "A walrus with blue ruffles." He nudged his brother with his elbow to get him to join in his chant: "Baby walrus, baby walrus, baby walrus."

"Yeah," Willie said, "It looks like you have a diaper on with that ruffle. You're a walrus that waddles in a diaper! If you guys thought you saw ghosts last night, well don't worry, this will scare them away!"

I felt my face turn redder and hotter. It felt like I had instant sunburn. I had just had it with them this time.

"I can't stand you two," I blurted out. "You have to ruin everything!"

I grabbed my little pack and called to Ming, and turned away from them and ran down the trail, with Ming running behind me.

"Bridget, wait!" Anna hollered. "Just stay with Gracey," I shouted back. "I want to be alone."

I just wanted to get away from them. Why did they have to ruin everything? Oh, how I hated that bathing suit. Now I didn't want anyone to see me. Ever. I ran for a long time, just wanting to get away. The trail was narrow and I had to watch for roots sticking up in the path.

The whole time I ran, hot tears stung my eyes. Finally, I had a pain

in my side and I had to slow down. I saw all these special things on the trail, like a tree growing on top of a boulder, and its trunk was curved like a dancer. I saw fungus, moss, and a slant of light through the trees. But nothing was making me feel better, and when I realized that, I felt more tears come. So I started running again, further and further. But the tears made my eyes blurry, and the next thing you know I stubbed my toe on a rock. This time I really cried, and bent down and grabbed my foot.

Now I truly felt miserable from head to toe. I knew I should have put on my sneakers before walking in the woods, but I had just wanted to get far away from those guys. I was even mad at my mother right now for buying that stupid bathing suit. I dragged myself over to the edge of the trail. I just wanted to be away from everybody. Maybe that's how Noah John Rondeau felt, I thought. Maybe he was sick of people and that's why he became a hermit. He suddenly seemed to me like he must have been the smartest man in the whole world.

Not far off, a little below the trail, I saw a beautiful bed of moss. It was a little out of sight, and that's exactly what I wanted. I could hear the roar of water again, and I could finally see the upper falls.

Ming and I went and sat on the moss. It was soft. I petted my puppy. She was soft, too. She put her head on my leg and looked up at me. She always knows when I am sad. I lay down, and put her next to me and held her leash. The moss was so soft, cool, and fluffy. It was like a fairy bed. From here, I could see the upper falls really well. This set of falls was shaped like a horseshoe. It seemed even faster than the lower falls. At the bottom, the water circled around widely in this one spot, instead of tumbling everywhere like the lower falls. I knew that was called an eddy. The water was white on top from the foam that was made by the rushing water.

I listened to the sound of the falls, and it was so nice. There were no other sounds, just pure water running over rocks. The water seemed sure of itself. I wished I felt that way.

The warm sun touched my face as I listened to the falls. It reminded me of the violins. One time my mother took me to Albany to hear a symphony, because she likes classical music and she likes to go to a city sometimes, especially in the winter when she gets cabin fever. That means you get sick of staying inside the house all winter. Even though she gets lost every time we drive in the city, gets mad at herself, and shouts in the car because she gets nervous, she always manages to finally find the way and calm down. She says getting lost whenever she travels outside the Adirondacks is a sure sign that she's been in the woods too long and has to get out.

When we got to the orchestra hall to see the symphony, I couldn't believe how beautiful the building was where the musicians played. The walls had paintings of angels and people in beautiful, lacy dresses. And high, high up on a ceiling, there were paintings of clouds and they looked so real and filled with light. There was also a gorgeous chandelier with a gazillion prisms. Once the lights dimmed, though, all I remember is being surprised at all the violinists on the stage. I couldn't believe how many there were. And they all wore black. Slowly the violinists began playing. And I remember that was the only sound, just that sweet sound of all those bows on all those strings. Different sections played different notes, and they all melted into each other. I felt like it was a big blanket of soft sound around me, and I fell asleep on my mother's shoulder.

I remember that I couldn't even think about another sound, except the violins. And that's what the sound of the falls was like to me now. All that water going over each different rock made different sounds but it was still all one sound. And I didn't have to think about anything else except that one sound, and it was nice enough that it filled my whole mind and I forgot about my toe, the boys, and my bathing suit. I just thought about the falls.

And then I drifted off to sleep on the moss.

Chapter Eleven

Dangerous Falls Ahead

When I woke up, I thought I heard a loud splash. But my eyes opened slowly. I guess I'd really taken a good nap. I looked around me, trying to remember where I was. Ming started licking my face. She always knows when I'm awake.

At first, I was a little afraid to sit up. It was getting late in the afternoon, and the sun was not directly overhead anymore. It was cooler. What if that splash had been the Lost Channel creature, coming over the falls? What if I sat up, and the creature saw me? Lying down, I was quite safe. No one could see me from the river or from the trail unless they were really looking for me. But then I started thinking that maybe the hermit's ghost had heard me say how I understood him, and so he thought I was ready to join him and he was coming to get me.

The thought made me feel stiff, like I couldn't move.

Any thoughts are possible when you're in the woods by yourself, even if the sun is still out. There's something about just being among the trees. Your thoughts change.

After a few minutes, I started wondering why the others weren't looking for me. Well, maybe I had just taken a short nap, after all. I hoped my dad wasn't worried or anything. I figured I better get back and find the others. But what about that splash I had heard?

I stretched, and looked around carefully as I sat up. Then I glanced down at the water to see what the noise had been.

Something was twirling around in the water! I leaned closer to look. It was someone in a life preserver, swirling around and around in the eddy below the falls. I could see a head bent to one side, and then I recognized the long, blonde hair. It was Danielle! It was the girl from New York City.

She was slowly turning around in the eddy, going around in the same circle over and over. I wondered why she wasn't swimming and kicking. It seemed like she could be stuck there forever if no one got her out.

"Danielle!" I shouted, cupping my hands over my mouth to help carry my voice over the noise of the falls. "Danielle!"

She didn't answer, or look up. Quickly, I called to Ming, grabbed my pack, and made my way down the rocks and embankments to get to this one big rock near the bottom of the falls. Danielle must have been sitting on the rock. But what could have happened?

Then I remembered the bracelet. It was in the outer pocket of my pack. Danielle is a diabetic; she must have gone into shock and fallen off the rock.

I told Ming to stay, and left her on the rock and waded into the water. It wasn't that deep, but the current was very strong. I was nervous and I dug my fingers into a crack in the big rock with one hand, stretching my other arm out toward Danielle. I didn't want to get swept into the eddy. I kept my legs steady by pressing down hard on my bare feet. The water was cool. I reached out as far as I dared."

"Danielle!" I shouted, waiting for her to swirl closer to me. "Danielle?"

There was still no answer.

Finally, as she circled toward me in the water, I lunged forward and grabbed the top of her life jacket, and then I put my arm under her neck and slowly pulled her out of the eddy and back to the rock. She wasn't heavy at all in the water, although I had to tug hard to move both of us against the current. I was glad we didn't have far to go. Once I held her against the rock, though, I realized I had no way to get her out of the water and onto the rock. I couldn't lift her by myself.

I held onto the rock with one hand, and held Danielle with my other arm. We were out of the fast moving water, at least.

I was breathing fast and hard. It was tough to think, and when I did, all I could come up with was, what should I do next? What? Would we both be stuck here? I felt so scared all of a sudden. I knew I had to just think about the next step to take. I thought about all the things I had learned about juvenile diabetes from my classmate's report. I remembered that some diabetics need regular shots of insulin because it helps their body process their high levels of sugar. But with other diabetics, if their sugar is too low, sometimes they can get really weak and go into a coma.

That must be what happened to Danielle. She sure seemed like she was in a coma. So, I needed to give her something with sugar. What? Then I remembered that I had juice boxes in my pack. They were still there from lunch.

I gently pushed Danielle up against a wide crack in the rock to hold her in place better, and then quickly reached up with the other hand to grab my pack, which luckily I had dropped at the edge of the rock. I reached in and found a little box of orange juice.

It was kind of hard to open with one hand, so I ripped the flap open with my teeth.

"Danielle?" I said. "I'm going to give you some juice."

I tilted her head back, and opened her mouth some more with my hand. Then I poured a little bit of juice in it. She coughed at first, and then swallowed. I waited. Very slowly, she opened her eyes. I looked at her and poured in some juice, and she swallowed it all. I kept giving her more until she finished the whole box.

She looked sort of sleepy, and not sure what was going on. She winced, and took her right arm and held onto her other arm with it. That's when I noticed that her left arm looked kind of funny. It seemed to hang there. I wondered if it was broken.

"Danielle, it's me. Remember, Bridget, you know, from the camp-site the other night?"

She nodded, but didn't talk. But at least she was awake now.

I decided I'd better shout for help.

"Anna!" I hollered. "Dad! Somebody help!" It was hard to hear anything above the roar of the falls. But I knew I had to do something. I knew we both couldn't keep standing in the water. I couldn't lift her out of the water by myself, especially if she had a broken arm and couldn't help lift herself.

I looked at Ming, right into her coal black eyes. She looked back at me.

"Go get Anna!" I said. "Ming, go get Anna." I pointed up the trail. "Go get her!"

I pointed up the hill again. Ming looked at me with a tilt to her head and a question in her eyes, as if wondering why I wasn't coming, too.

"Go get Anna!" I said. "Anna has a treat!"

I was afraid to let her go, since she'd only been on this trail once. But she's a good sniffer, and because she knows Anna so well, I knew she would understand my command, especially if there was going to be a treat for her. She'd go anywhere for a treat, which was usually a little dog bone, flavored with meat.

Ming raced up the hill and onto the trail. When she got to the top, she stopped and looked at me again, tilting her head to the right side.

"Go get Anna!" I said. "Anna has a treat!"

Off she ran.

I waited in the water with Danielle. I stroked her hair.

"Don't worry," I said. "Help is on the way. I think you got really weak and slipped into a coma and fell off the rock. I know you have diabetes because I found your medical bracelet back in the lean-to the other night. Has it been a long time since you'd eaten?"

She nodded her head yes.

I wanted to keep talking to her so she didn't get scared. I like to have people do that when I'm scared. If there's no one around to talk to when I feel that way, or if I just can't sleep for some reason, then I just read a book. It's kind of like having someone talk to me, too.

I told Danielle all about how Anna and I had camped last night, with Gracey, too, and how we had built a big fire and did a ghost dance around it. I just figured that since I had tourist information about her, she should have some about me. I told her we wanted to talk to the ghosts and let them know everything was okay here in the woods. I told her about Willie and Charlie scaring us, and then how today they had been teasing me about my bathing suit, and that's why I was on the trail by myself today.

I also told her how much I liked her bathing suit. Under the life jacket, I could see that it was neon green and white striped. It was definitely a cool bathing suit. I bet she got it in New York City.

Danielle looked tired, but she smiled when I told her about the ghost dance, and when I told her I liked her bathing suit. I also told her the others weren't too far away, and help was on the way.

She just shivered.

Finally, I heard my name being called. I hollered back as loud as I could, shouting "Hello! I'm here!" Then I turned my head, and saw Anna, Gracey, Peter, Willie, Charlie, and their cousin Jamie. Boy, was I happy to see everybody! They scrambled down to us.

Jamie took off his boots and got in the water. He looked at Danielle's arm.

"I think it's broken," he said. "And she's shivering. Let's get her out."

Jamie held Danielle from one side, and I held the other. Together we lifted her up slowly to Willie and Charlie, who were kneeling on the rock above us. They gently lowered her onto the rock, being careful not to jar her arm. Jamie and I held her legs while they guided her onto the flat part of the rock. Anna held her head.

Then Jamie and I got out of the water. I was feeling chilly now.

He still had on his backpack from the horseback ride, and he pulled out a little saddle blanket he used for the horses and wrapped Danielle in it.

"I've been a guide for about five years now," he said, "taking people on horseback rides. I had to take a couple rescue courses to get my guide license. When a person is sick or injured, you have to keep them warm so they don't into shock."

"Where are our dads?" I asked.

"They were still fishing when we left," Jamie said. "We were already part-way up the trail when we spotted Ming and she started barking and running down the trail back toward you. We were coming to find you, but we sure didn't know there was trouble. We were looking for you so the boys could apologize to you. You see, when I got to the lower falls today to join Willie and Charlie for fishing, Gracey and Anna told me about the boys picking on you and how you'd run off. I didn't want to worry your father, so we all came to get you and make sure you're okay."

Willie pushed the toe of his hiking boots into the rock, like he was nervous. "I really didn't mean to make you that mad," he said. "I was just teasing, you know. I'm sorry."

"Yeah, me, too," Charlie said.

"Thanks," I said.

"Okay, Bridget," Jamie said, "You and Anna stay here with Danielle. Here's some water for her," he said, pulling out a thermos. "She needs to drink. It's important that she doesn't get dehydrated, which means a person doesn't have enough liquids in their body. Willie and Charlie and Peter, you come with me."

"Yeah," Willie said, "let's go to that old barn next to the ranger cabin. The ranger said there's some old doors in there and we can use one to carry Danielle out."

"Yeah," Peter said, "That's how they rescued the ranger one time. I remember, he told us at the campfire. Just before Charlie puked."

"We'll stop and get your dads on the way down the trail," Jamie said to Anna, Gracey, and me. "And if we're lucky, the ranger will be there and he can help us. And I'm sure we'll run into your parents, Danielle. They're probably looking all over for you."

Danielle nodded.

"I know it's a long way back to the cabin, but hurry," I said. "There's something I haven't told you that none of you know. Danielle's a diabetic. I think she was in a coma."

"Have you given her something with sugar?" Jamie asked.

94

"I gave her juice," I said.

"Good job," Jamie said. "And listen, as soon as we're gone, get those wet clothes off Danielle and put some dry ones on her. I've got a long t-shirt and that will have to do for now. Bridget, you should get dry, too. Look in your packs, girls, and see what you can find."

He took his t-shirt off and left it with us.

"Be careful of her arm!" he shouted back to us as he walked up the trail with Willie, Charlie, and Peter.

Anna and I carefully lifted Danielle's head and took off her life preserver. Then we peeled off her wet bathing suit and put Jamie's dry t-shirt on her. It looked like a nightgown it was so long. Then we covered her with the saddle blanket. She seemed to be dozing again.

I dug in my pack, found one of my towels, and put it under her head.

"Hey, I just remembered I grabbed your t-shirt from the rock at the lower falls when we left to come get you," Anna said.

"Good," I said. I was starting to shiver, too.

I peeled off my suit and toweled dry. Then I put on my t-shirt that Anna had rescued. She also had a pair of shorts in her pack, and gave them to me to wear. I wrapped a towel around my legs to keep them warm.

Gracey sat on the rock next to us. We were like four birds in a rock nest, huddled together.

"It's so lucky that you found her!" Anna said. "Where did you go anyway?"

"Oh, I was so mad at Willie and Charlie!" I said. "I just ran off because I'm sick of them teasing me. And I fell asleep on a bed of moss, but I don't think I slept long because I woke up when I heard this splash. I guess it was Danielle falling in the water."

"I like your bathing suit!" Gracey said. "I don't think they should pick on you."

"Well, Gracey, I'll tell you what. I'm going to save this bathing suit for you. When you get bigger, you can have it. And it will still be like new, because I probably won't wear it very much," I said.

Gracey smiled. I could tell she looked forward to having my bathing suit.

"Danielle has a pretty bathing suit," Gracey said. "But do you think she's going to be okay?"

"Help is on the way," I said. "At least she's out of the water now, and dry. I'm sure the ranger can help take her to a hospital. He said they did it for him that time he got hurt."

"Hey," Gracey said, "now you're going to have to make up a verse about this to add to your Adirondack song."

"I hope you'll help me," I said. "For now, why don't I teach you the song as it is now, and then later, when we're out of this mess, we can add the new verse?"

I sang one verse, and they repeated it until they had it memorized. Then I went on to the next verse. It took our mind off waiting and worrying.

Danielle was still shivering, even in the blanket.

Chapter Twelve

Tourist Information

Finally, we heard shouts, and looked up. Everybody was there, coming toward us. Ranger Michael and our dads were carrying the door, and behind them came Danielle's parents. Jamie, Willie, Charlie, and Peter followed behind, and they were soaked with sweat. They must have run the whole way.

They all climbed down to the rock, and Danielle's parents rushed to her and hugged her.

Ranger Michael told us we needed to get Danielle out of the woods quickly so he could take her by boat to Axton Landing, where his truck was parked. From there, he would take her to the hospital.

"We have to watch out for hypothermia," the ranger said. "That's where a person's body temperature drops from being exposed too long. It's very dangerous. You kids were very smart to get her into dry clothes and cover her up."

"Jamie helped us," I said.

The ranger took a blanket from his backpack and wrapped Danielle in it. He checked her pulse by holding her wrist, and he checked her eyes for movement. Then he unfolded a temporary brace that he had in his backpack, and put her arm inside it.

"By the time we get back to the cabin it'll nearly be dark," he said. "But I've got a light on my boat and I know this river really well. Danielle will have to stay well covered and lying on the door, but her mom and dad can hold onto her. I'll put the door on top of the seats in the boat."

Ranger Michael bent down to examine her further. "Her mom and dad told me on the way here about her diabetes. I think she walked a lot further than she had planned on. My guess is that she got tired and shaky, sat on the rock and went into diabetic shock and fell into the water. She probably rolled over onto her arm as she fell, and the weight of her body against the rock, combined with twisting as she fell, is what broke it. Luckily for her, she was wearing her life preserver. She just ferried around this eddy. It's a good thing she wasn't at the lower falls; it would have pulled her under."

Danielle's mother looked like she was going to throw up.

"I was napping up there on the moss," I said, "and I heard a splash. But she didn't answer me, and she wouldn't wake up when I reached her and pulled her to the rock. I knew she was a diabetic, because I found her medical bracelet back at the lean-to." I pulled it out of my pack and gave it to Danielle's mom. "When she wouldn't wake up, I gave her some orange juice, because this girl in my class has diabetes and she has to eat or drink something if she gets weak because of low blood sugar."

"We didn't realize she didn't have any food with her or anything,"

Danielle's dad said. "Come to think of it, she didn't eat much breakfast. Then later, she just said she wanted to go for a little walk. We spent the day up here yesterday, so I knew that she knew the way. We always have her wear her life jacket around water, because of her diabetes. Doctors have told us not to baby her because it's important that she have regular activities. So, that's what we do. We just try to take extra care that she's protected."

"Well, it's a good thing you do," Ranger Michael said. "That life jacket and this girl here helped save her life."

He pointed right at me. I felt warm inside.

Danielle's mother leaned over and stroked Danielle's face, and then lifted her head up and gave her some water. Then she gave her some crackers.

Then she looked right at me.

"Thank you, Bridget, so much, for helping her," she said.

"Oh, you're welcome," I said proudly.

I asked the ranger for some water from his thermos, and I poured it into the thermos cup for Ming. She drank the whole cup. Then I picked her up and told her what a good dog she is. Slowly, we started up the hill and onto the path, a whole string of us.

Gracey said her job would be to keep any mosquitoes off Danielle, and she got a branch full of leaves and waved it over Danielle as we walked. Danielle was more awake now, and she smiled at Gracey. Ranger Michael and Danielle's dad held up the front of the door, and our dads held up the back.

In some spots, the trail was narrow and we had to walk more slowly and carefully. Also, there were large tree roots sticking out in some places, so that meant we had to be step around them or over them. Anna and I were out front, watching for the roots so we could alert the guys carrying Danielle to be careful.

Peter said he wanted to be the lookout person, so he went up front with Danielle's mom, and Anna and I dropped back and walked behind everybody. Even though it was getting late in the day, it was still hot. Ranger Michael and Danielle's dad had dark spots of sweat soaking through their shirts in the middle of their backs. I thought it looked like they were carrying little lakes on their back.

It took us a long time to get back. Peter kept announcing to everyone that he was really hungry. I swatted deer flies away from my head, and wished we were at the end of the trail. At least the smell of the cedars and the balsam trees was comforting as we walked.

Finally, we passed by the lower falls and I knew we were almost back to the cabin. The trail was twisty again, and then came out on the main trail. The cabin was off to the right.

The guys put the door down outside the cabin while Ranger Michael went inside to get his flashlight and some other supplies. He let us come in and have some water to drink and go to the bathroom, while Danielle's parents waited outside with her. I splashed cool water on my face from the bathroom sink. We all had a lot of bug bites on our necks.

The ranger picked up the microphone from his radio and called a dispatcher.

"I have an eleven-year-old girl, a diabetic, possible broken arm. Fell into the river after apparently going into diabetic shock. I will be transporting her to Axton Landing and from there to the hospital in Saranac Lake. Please radio the hospital and let them know we are on our way."

We were standing in his kitchen. I saw an old picture of an elderly woman, and the name under it said Mother Johnson. I asked the ranger if that was his mother, and he laughed.

"No," he said. "A long time ago there were lodges here at the falls. People used to come through here all the time on hunting and fishing trips. Mother Johnson was most famous for making big breakfasts for people who stayed at the lodge. Her specialty was pancakes."

"Do you have a specialty?" Peter asked. "Because I sure am hungry."

"Well," Ranger Michael said, lifting the lid of his faded green cap from his head and wiping the sweat from his forehead, "My specialty is homemade waffles, but right now I have a little girl to help and I can't be cooking. But you never know, maybe another time . . ."

He ruffled Peter's hair. Then we all helped move Danielle down to the river, where the ranger's boat was tied up to a dock. We loaded Danielle and the door carefully onto the seats.

"Are you okay?" Ranger Michael asked Danielle, smiling, as he sat down next to her on the seat in the back of the boat. It wasn't a big boat, and the motor was the kind with a handle on it that you steered by moving it left or right from behind you. He sat in front of the engine, with

the handle to one side of him. Danielle's father was in the front, holding a big flashlight.

"Yup," Danielle said, "but it's getting dark. How are we going to get down the river with just a flashlight?"

"Don't you worry about that," he said. "I know every nook and cranny of this river. I even have names for every bend in the river to be sure I know where I am. There's Hanging Pine Corner, Hemlock Hill, Chipmunk Crossing—that's where I saw a couple of baby chipmunks swimming across the river one day—Cedar Bend, and Crooked Limb Corner. You'll like that one. There's a huge balsam there with a giant crooked branch that hooks out over the river and then reaches up tall into the sky. And then there's Lightning Bolt Bend. Why, one time there was a thunder and lightning storm up here and you could hear the thunder rolling for miles. Well, I was sitting on the porch of the cabin and I heard the most awful crack I ever heard in my life. I thought the mountains were splitting in two. The next morning I came down the river and found this giant tree had been split right in two. One half was still standing and the other fell backwards and knocked down four other trees as it fell. It was really something."

Danielle smiled again.

I could tell he liked telling a good story, just like my dad did. If he didn't have to get Danielle to the hospital, I bet he could've talked for a lot longer and told us many more stories about his adventures living at Raquette Falls. I wished he were telling us stories in the morning, while we were eating homemade waffles, instead of at night, when he was about to leave us at the falls after a long, scary day.

"Well, good luck. I'm glad you guys are in safe hands," my dad said.

The ranger called good-bye to us, and then pulled the cord that started the engine, and away they went. We waved from the dock. The little boat disappeared into the darkening evening around the bend in the river, and they were out of sight.

Chapter Thirteen

Heading Home

That night, we didn't even build a fire. We were all so tired we just climbed into the lean-to together. Our dads moved the little tent Anna and I had slept in next to the lean-to, and they slept there with Willie and Charlie. After last night, Anna and I didn't want to sleep alone. Just before falling asleep, though, we all shared our tourist information. Mine, of course, was that Danielle is a diabetic. Gracey said she found out that Danielle's mom hates perfume. Anna said she found out that Danielle's favorite food is pepperoni, but chicken cooked with lemon makes her throw up. Peter said he saw Danielle's dad climb out of the tent early in the morning on his knees, which made him look really short. His face was full of whiskers and he looked just like an old hermit.

"Oh, no," I said. "I can't fall asleep thinking about that old hermit again!"

"Hey," Gracey said, sitting up. "Just one more thing. You remember that your dad said the hermit made up his own code for a whole language while he was alone all those years?"

"Yeah," I said.

"Well, let's make up a code we can share with Danielle!" Gracey said. "You guys always have secret ideas. This one is mine. But I'll share it with you. We can write to Danielle with the code."

"How will we get her address?" I asked.

"Well, if Ranger Michael is back tomorrow before we leave, maybe he'll have Danielle's address, for his records, you know," Anna said.

"That's a great idea!" I said.

"Hey," Peter said. "Let's call it the Lost Channel Code."

We all put our hands on top of each other again, making a pact. Then we raised our hands in the air, and then we lay back down and fell asleep.

I didn't hear anyone snore.

The next morning, I woke up and put on my bathing suit for a quick swim before we started our last day's paddle. I didn't care any more about Willie and Charlie or what they thought about my suit. I'd just wear it if I felt like it. And maybe I'd get a babysitting job soon and I'd save my money and buy a cool bathing suit of my own. Besides, Anna and I had made Willie and Charlie eat bark. I smiled at the thought of all that wood in Willie's teeth. I knew, too, that we'd seen stuff they hadn't at that campfire, and that was something special they couldn't take away from us.

When we were walking back from our swim, the ranger hollered out from his cabin.

"Hey, come here, you guys!" he said, smiling.

We raced up to the cabin, eager to hear about Danielle.

"Danielle's fine," he said. "I stayed with her at the hospital for a while. Sure enough, she has a broken arm and they put it in a cast. She's going to stay there a day until they're sure she's okay with her diabetes and everything. They have her on some medicine. I came back to the falls first thing this morning, as soon as it was daybreak. I love going up the river early in the morning when all is quiet. I scared a couple of baby ducks, though, when I came around a corner. They went paddling away as fast as could be!"

"Hey, something smells really good," Gracey said. She and Peter are always hungry. I think that's why they're best friends.

Ranger Michael smiled.

"I have a surprise for you. Come on out on the porch," he said.

There he had set up a table, and he had a stack of waffles staying warm under an upside down pot.

"Oh, boy!" Peter said.

Both our dads sure did look happy. I don't think they wanted to cook this morning.

We sat down and ate waffles with real maple syrup. It was the best breakfast I ever had. From the porch, we could hear the sound of the falls, and I thought again of the violins. It was a beautiful sound.

"Shh!" I said suddenly to Willie, who was talking.

I pointed, and as everyone looked, we saw a mother deer and her fawn not far from the cabin, nibbling on some food in the meadow. They were so sweet. I thought of the time Gracey and I were lost in the woods last winter, and we saw the deer. Ever since then, I just know somehow when you see a deer it means everything is going to be all right. It's a message from the forest.

Just then, Ranger Michael reached into his back pocket.

"I nearly forgot," he said. "Here's Danielle's address. She wants you guys to write to her, okay?"

We all smiled. I just knew it would work out.

"Sure thing," I said, taking the piece of paper.

Finally, it was time to go, and we said good-bye to the ranger and thanked him for breakfast. Willie, Charlie, and Jamie headed out to their horses and rode out of the woods, and we climbed into our canoes.

The day's paddling was nice. The river looked dark and mysterious in some spots, and light and sandy in others. It looked golden sometimes. There were bends and turns everywhere. In some places, the banks of the river were high and sandy from where the water was higher in the spring-time. In other spots, the trees grew right out from the banks, hanging over the river as if leaning over to get a drink. I like the hemlocks a lot.

As we came around one bend, I sucked in my breath when I saw, in a marshy area off the side of the river, a great blue heron. They are tall, beautiful birds and they are very patient. They stand for a very long time, watching and waiting for fish. They have long beaks and thin feathers that hang from their neck. Maybe they are Indian birds, I thought.

When Anna's paddle hit the side of her canoe, the bird suddenly took off; its long straight legs sticking out behind its body. I love to watch herons fly.

A little further down the river, as we came closer to Axton Landing, we saw a mother duck and six, seven, eight, nine—no, twelve—ducklings! The mother had them moving so fast away from us that they looked like tiny motorboats, churning up the water behind them as they paddled fast and furious out of our way. We were all laughing. I wondered if they were the same ducks Ranger Michael had seen earlier that morning.

Finally, a few more bends, a few more hemlocks and maples and patches of sunlight in the water and through the trees, and we were at Axton Landing.

Our moms were already there! They were sitting on shore in little folding chairs, talking and swatting bugs away from their head. Anna and Gracey's mom held Gretchen in her lap. The baby had on a sunbonnet.

We got out of the boats carefully, jumping from canoe to shore, because Anna was sure she saw a leech swimming in the water. Ugh.

I gave my mom a big hug. She hugged me back. Then she scooped up Ming, who was jumping up for a hug of her own.

"Oh, we have so much to tell you! Wait until you hear everything that happened," I said.

"Somehow, I knew you were going to have an adventure," she said, smiling.

She helped my dad and I unload our boat, and everyone was talking at once telling her about Danielle and the accident and swimming in the chute and the skits around the fireplace that first night.

My dad looked at my mom and smiled.

"You know, we saw a sign on the river that said Dangerous Falls

Ahead. And that's exactly what happened! Danielle had a dangerous fall!" he said.

My mom grinned. "You and your signs," she said.

"Hey," Gracey said, tugging my mom's sleeve. "I saw fireflies from the fairies. I could see them right through the tent."

Anna and I looked at each other, startled. Had she been awake while we did our ceremony, after all?

My mom took Gracey's hand and brought her to our car. "Come here, girls," she said to Anna and I. She opened the door and pulled out a new quilt from a bag on the back seat that she had started while she was at her workshop. As she unfolded it carefully, I could see that she had hand stitched it with a design of fireflies. The background was dark purple like a night sky, and she had stitched little stars with silver thread. Toward the bottom of the quilt, she had used pieces of brightly colored fabrics with all kinds of designs to show wildflowers growing. The golden yellow fireflies weaved in among the flowers. They lit up the quilt. They almost looked like they were moving.

And there, in the bottom corner, peeking out from some flowers, she had created three little fairies out of fabric! She had made their wings out of shiny silver material that had specks of white in it. My mom always put something extra in her quilts. Sometimes you have to find things she's hidden in the design.

We all squealed we were so excited.

"I made three fairies in honor of my three favorite girls," she said, hugging us. "This is the project I did in my quilting class this week. I still have some finishing work to do on it. My instructor said I am very good. I learned so much, and made new friends, just like you guys did meeting Danielle!"

"It's beautiful, Mom," I said.

"It's for you," she said.

I smiled very big, as big as the widest turn in the Raquette River. I turned to show my dad the quilt, when Gracey tugged my sleeve.

"Hey," she said. "Don't forget to tell your mom that Charlie threw up, too!"

Anna and I looked at each other and burst out laughing. Well, we promised him we wouldn't tell he threw up, but we weren't the ones spilling the secret, were we. I knew though, that no one else should know, if that's what Charlie really wanted.

"Gracey," I said, leaning down. "Let's not tell anyone else, okay. We don't want to make Charlie feel bad, okay?"

"Okay," she said.

Before we each got into our family cars, I gave Gracey a big hug good-bye and thanked her for all her chocolate somemores and for being a good secret keeper about our ceremony. She got in the car, and then Anna and I hugged good-bye.

"Anna," I said. "We really did see something by that fire when we had our ceremony, didn't we?" I wanted to be sure I hadn't dreamed that, too, because it sure had seemed so real at the time. But since then, with Danielle's fall and everything, I was beginning to wonder if maybe we hadn't just imagined that other stuff.

"I think we saw something for sure," she said. "I was hoping you were sure, too, though. I mean, I was wondering, do you think it might have just been smoke from the fire making funny shapes, or some night clouds? You know how you're always picking shapes out of clouds?"

I shook my head back and forth.

"No way," I said. "That much I know. It wasn't clouds. And if you agree that you saw something, I know I wasn't just imagining things. Because I remember shapes—people shapes. And they weren't like clouds."

She looked relieved.

"Me, too," she said. "But I just wanted to be sure you didn't think I was being crazy or something."

"No way," I said again, hugging her good-bye. "We saw some spirits. And I bet the ghosts are still talking about it back at the Lost Channel!"

About the Author . . .

Liza Frenette has many adventures in the waters and woods of the Adirondack Mountains. She lived there for thirty years, first in Tupper Lake while trying to grow up, and then in Saranac Lake with her daughter, Jasmine. Albany is now their home.

Although Liza has paddled from Long Lake to Tupper Lake several times, she decided long ago that the swimming was the best part of the trip. In the summer she likes to go water-hopping; some favorite spots are the Raquette River, Claudia's Pond-In-The-Rain, Lake George, Warners Lake, Cape Cod, and Chapel Pond. For her, the highlight of researching this book was swimming in the chute at Raquette Falls with the real Ranger Mike, Ranger Ben, Gracey, Megan, Gary, the illustrator Jane Gillis, and Ming, the wonder dog—who is very real.

About the Illustrator . . .

Born and raised in the Adirondacks, Jane Gillis had many adventures on the water and in the woods with her siblings and cousins. She and her sister, Barbara, started canoeing in Girl Scout Camp, and as they got more experienced, they entered canoe races in the region. Going down the Raquette was a favorite canoe trip. Jane says, "It is thrilling to make drawings for a story that could be one of my own adventures."

As an artist and calligrapher, Jane employs watercolor, gouache, pen, pencil, and her imagination. Her subject matter includes figures, landscapes, and words.

She is grateful to her large family and many friends who have helped her guide her canoe through the river of life.